The Final Shal

By David Midd

Introduction

In a confusion of fact and fiction, a South Korean "chaos entrepreneur", supported by a group of former Cheka terrorists and funded by a Russian Oligarch, sets out to pressurise California to leave the United States of America.

Our main character and reluctant hero (who has a contentious surname and a confusing first name) becomes embroiled in a story that includes a massacre in an isolated pub on the north coast of Scotland; plotting in the exotic Flying Bird Tea Shop in Seoul; politics in the Palace of Westminster, California, Washington and Montreux; a gun battle on Lake Geneva - all against a true backcloth of the world failing to respond to some of the most testing challenges it has ever encountered.

The Final Shah Mat

By David Middleton

First published 2014

Author's Notes

This book is a weave of fact and fiction. All the characters and the events are pure fiction and drawn from my imagination though most of the places in the story do exist. However, all the information about the state of our planet and issues to do with sustainable development are, to the best of my knowledge, accurate. Conversely, I have no idea if California will ever depart company with the USA! However, in my lifetime the Berlin Wall has gone, the Soviet Union has collapsed, apartheid has gone from South Africa and Northern Ireland is by no means as dangerous a place as it used to be. So anything is possible!

All the people in the book are fictitious. However, everything I wrote about Brian Kemp is based on the astonishing Professor Tony Marmont and what he has achieved with his farming and Beacon Energy enterprises in Leicestershire - not Warwickshire as I have them. And as with the fictitious Brian Kemp, Tony really has provided financial support to UK and USA universities - has his own jet helicopter - and is seeking to produce an answer to the global energy crisis.

The sad story of Sandy Macaulay of the tremendous PURE energy project on Unst in the Shetland Islands is one not to dwell on but to simply acknowledge Sandy's drive and enthusiasm that led this fantastic project until he disappeared off the island. I am delighted PURE still runs as an acknowledgement of Sandy's vision and drive.

I have had a love affair with the north coast of Scotland for many years, retreating there to a crofter's cottage we owned near the village of Bettyhill, about half way between John O'Groats and Cape Wrath. I guess this part of the book is a little autobiographical as are my experiences of working in the Palace of Westminster, the Flying Bird Tea Shop in Seoul and in Montreux.

Sadly what is not fiction is the appalling state of our planet and the way we are abusing it. If this novel does anything to stimulate people to respond to the challenges and responsibilities we confront it will have done what I hoped it might.

About Me

Always a keen writer, I was given a chance at the age of 20 to become a news reporter on the weekly local newspaper, the Walsall Observer. I spent a few years in local newspapers and radio before becoming a motor sport photo journalist. Via time in commercial PR, I moved into the world of exhibitions and conferences which took me across Europe, Japan and the USA. In 1988 I had my "green epiphany" standing on a bridge in Pittsburgh. In 1991 I helped launch the MEBC, a business group dedicated to the subject of sustainable development. I became its CEO. I was Secretary General of TURF - The Urban Renewal Foundation. I later also added the role of CEO of the UK branch of the World Business Council for Sustainable Development to my activities. I retired from these responsibilities in 2013.

© Copyright

All copyrights reserved to David Middleton
2014

Dedication

This book is dedicated to my Mom who elected to adopt me when medical advice was telling her not to. She gave me a chance in life that is an unpayable debt. It is also in memory of Pat and Les who we miss badly.

I also dedicate the book to my TEABAGs – "The Editorial Appraisal of Book Action Group" consisting of my long suffering wife Jennie, great encourager Debbie Dorman, creative daughter Caroline, supporting son Anthony, and long-time friend Kevin Walsh, . They gave me encouragement and guidance during the writing process. Also a variety of others who helped after the book was written.

Preface

I have spent more than 20 years promoting sustainable development, a set of values which seeks to ensure my generation passes this planet onto the next generation in some sound order. Against that objective we will sadly fail. But many of us who believe in the principles of sustainable development in which financial, social and environmental values are equal have thought that to get the subject woven into the script of a TV soap would be a great way to promote sustainable development to the general population.

Instead of doing that I have weaved truth and fiction into a story of espionage and political intrigue that seeks to entertain but also promote sustainable development values. It will not only satisfy my personal ambitions to have a book published but will, I hope, carry the sustainable development story to a wider audience than I have ever reached to date.

The Final Shah Mat

Chapter 1

The rust pitted metal latch of the heavy wooden front door clattered and the door itself crashed open in an uncontrolled way as a lively gust of wind crossed the northern extremities of Caithness and battered the inn. The round dull brass door knob bashed against the wall and added yet another micro-inch to the indentation that gave evidence that this was far from being a rare happening. A cold blast of raw North Scottish coast night air swept into the inn's one and only room and swirled the near fog-like atmosphere – a heady mix of peat and logs, fire smoke and alcohol.

The inn's proprietor, standing behind his bar with his body stooped forward, elbows on the bar top reading last week-end's Sunday paper, used his arms as well as his hands to stop his newspaper flying off in all directions as the intrusive wind sought to deny him his read. In the open hearth the fire surged, crackled and spat as if angered by this invasion as it was hit by a blast of bitterly cold air. The three bulb central light hanging from the ceiling swung wildly, casting jumping shadows across the room. A bearded, scruffy haired, aged but slim figured man with dishevelled and much faded trench coat, head topped with a dark blue woollen cap, sat at the edge of the bar. His layers of clothing seemed to defy any warmth was being generated by the fire. The old man did not let the assault on the tranquillity of the inn interrupt his contemplation of the half consumed pint of ale that sat before him. He remained, as ever, seemingly mesmerised by the liquor, his mind locked into years long past, and his body motionless except when in the act of bending the elbow to lift glass to mouth.

Time passes slowly and predictability dominates in this part of mainland UK, the last vestige of land before it gives way to the seemingly endless reaches of the North Sea. Indeed the slow tick of time passing is a high characteristic and an intrinsically essential element of the DNA of this rugged, beautiful and sometimes startling part of Scotland where the mountains, lochs and forests seem bigger than in any other part of the country. Many hold to the belief that the real Scotland only begins north of Inverness and this Caithness coastal area was a good two hours drive north of there. Just a little up the hill from where the inn stands, the view is stunning with - unless denied by sea mist or fog - the Orkney Isles visible across the water to the North East and the Western Highlands to the South West. This is unarguably an area of special grandiose and rugged beauty integrated into huge areas of sparse and expansive nothingness.

The lonely inn stands in almost solitary isolation on the most northerly main road of the country, the nearest other buildings being a line of cottages half a mile away. A rugged, four-square building in its grey hand cut stone structure, it is located on a hill and set back from the main road that links the two northern extremities of Scotland – John O'Groats to the East and Cape Wrath to the West. It provides service to the almost feudal local crofting community, a few outsider retirees and to passing tourists. Most times during the winter, it is in a state of near silence and virtually empty with life around it ticking on with a sense of quiet regularity, one slow day following another. On this cold, wet and blustery night, this routine regularity was to be rudely awakened.

The new arrival, dripping rain onto the uneven wooden floor and carrying a black hold-all over his shoulder and crash hat in his hand, bent instinctively as he passed under the low wooden ceiling beam. Many a stranger had been caught unexpectedly by this solid timber cross member but the new arrival, taller than six feet, lean and with long legs and wearing wet and shining motor cycle leathers, ducked. The damage to his forehead was nearly healed now but remained as testimony to the bloody ruthlessness of the encounter of his head with the heavily gnarled timber beam two days before when he first arrived at the inn. Somewhere, buried in the memory cells, was the pain. Instinct responded. He ducked.

"Toilet," he grunted. His English was good but the Eastern European accent undeniable. With a smile and a nod at the proprietor who was still preoccupied in trying to reassemble his newspaper, the motorcyclist crossed the bar and headed towards the sign that said ".. nts"- it having long ago lost its first two letters.

The proprietor nodded back without a word but thought what a dreadful evening it was outside for motorcycling. Not that the enormous number of foreign motorcyclists attracted to northern Scotland seemed to mind the weather. Like moths to a glowing light, they were drawn to the open, relatively traffic free roads and the outstanding scenery. And like moths against hot electric bulbs, they seemed to have an amazing ability to kill themselves every year - whatever the weather - in worrying numbers - on the fast and twisting, sheep littered tarmac strips that snake across the north coast. This rider, unusually not in the company of his delectable companion this evening, thought the proprietor, had been at the inn for a couple of days and seemed a jovial sort. He was very talkative even if language was an inhibitor to free flowing conversation. But that was not confined to Eastern European meeting English. It was equally problematical when some of the locals joined in. The proprietor was not local but had been at the inn long enough to have grown used to it all. He was now able to converse with those whose English seemed closer to Gaelic than the national tongue - even to Jimmie, the ancient character with the trench coach and woollen hat.

The proprietor did not look up again when the young man re-entered the bar which is why he did not see the silenced 9mm Makarov PB fire its high velocity cartridge with deadly accuracy at his heart. The bullet struck. The proprietor died. And before the woolly hat could turn to see what had happened, the beer drinker had received a cartridge to the forward part of the side of his head. The body of the proprietor, arms flaying, crashed backwards into the optics and stacked glasses at the rear of the bar, shattering many of them and sending a noisy cascade of broken glass to the floor along with the body. The ancient beer drinker simply slumped forward where he sat, blood from his haemorrhaging head colouring the ancient timbers of the bar top and mixing with the ale from his smashed glass.

The motorcyclist, older in years than his youthful appearance, was deadly accurate with the Makarov having used it as a frequent working tool ever since he retrieved it from a dead member of the Russian Spetsnaz who he had fought against briefly and unsuccessfully in the battle for the Chechen capital of Grozny. The then much younger mercenary freedom fighter had escaped the country in the chaotic ending to the conflict and the inevitable Russian victory. Since then, the Makarov had become the tool of his trade as he first went freelance then established his kill-to-order agency.

Now he strode quickly across the bar and fired a second subsonic bullet into the beer drinker, this time directly into his heart. At much the same time a distant voice – female – came from upstairs.

"Harry. You alright?"

This was not unexpected to the motorcyclist. A quick external reconnaissance of the inn before he had entered had shown that Barbara Arrowsmith was upstairs while her husband was in the bar with the one and only customer. He waited for the inevitable.

"Harry." The call came again, closer now. Then the sounds of creaking boards as Barbara Arrowsmith descended the stairs from above to find what the noise had been about and why her husband had not responded. Dressed in dark trousers and yellow jumper she made a cautionary entrance to the bar and took an intake of breath to scream at the sight of two male bodies and now serious amounts of blood around both corpses. But the scream never left her. But life did as the deadly Makarov spat again and the marksman, as professional as ever, hit his target at the optimum point. She too crashed to the floor in an ungainly heap, like a poleaxed puppet.

The motorcyclist moved quickly to the inn's front door, opened it and let in another leather clad figure. He shut the door, dropped the catch and slid the bolt. The second motorcyclist was female. Tall and shapely, as she removed her crash hat she released a cascade of blonde hair that fell down across her shoulders. Mr and Mrs Arrowsmith would have instantly recognised her as the motorcyclist's companion of the last few days.

"What a nice young girl," Barbara had said to her husband. He had nodded in agreement though his thoughts on the blonde girl were tainted by more lecherous considerations. This girl stirred a masculine lust in him that he thought had been dormant for far too long! His wife would have severely reprimanded him had she been able to read his mind. "Thank God she can't," he reassured himself. "Dirty old man," she would have said.

Without a word between them the two motorcyclists started a comprehensive, meticulous search of the inn from top to bottom. Being winter and a horrible night outside, their work was free from interruption which was as they expected. In their few days at the inn there had been no other overnight guests and no other visitors to the bar except the daily evening visit of the local with the woolly hat.

It was not neat work but it was complete. Not a cupboard or drawer was excluded from their efforts which left every room looking as if a bomb had exploded. Neatness was not a prerequisite of this process.

Three hours later the two donned their helmets and left. There was a pause before they drove off as the male of the two opened his iPhone, called up a number and said "we find nothing and we leave three discards. If there should have been a fourth, we don't know where it is". They climbed aboard the Yamaha and left the inn's car park with a flurry of stones, pebbles and mud. Little did they know as they headed through the blackness of the night and the bursts of driving rain towards Thurso, that coming towards them heading West in his black Porsche 911 Carrera Coupe was what the motorcyclist had described as "a fourth". They were yet to know that driving the Porsche was Gene Bond.

Chapter 2

The President was not just angry. He was raging. Any angrier and he would have been frothing at the mouth! It was a time for prudent people to be as far away as they could get. Target for his outburst was the unfortunate Carl Barker, the President's publicity advisor, who just happened to be in the wrong place at the wrong time. A friend of the President for years and eventually a guiding mentor on all the President's political campaigning, Barker had been widely adjudged to have been the principal instrument in the President winning the last election so as to enjoy a second term of office. A former newsman and latterly a publisher, Barker was squat and round - and bald, overweight and with cirrhosis. At this moment he was also extremely uncomfortable.

Driven by his rage, the President had virtually swept Barker up and headed at an uncompromising speed along the not inconsiderable distance from his study next to the Oval Office to the Vice President's office. People they encountered nodded in deference but stood aside, keen not to hinder the President's meteoric progress. His pace made Barker breathless. The political advisor's square little body and short legs tried desperately to keep up with the long-striding President and by the time they reached their destination Barker was red faced, sweaty, puffing vigorously and seriously damp inside his shirt collar and across his forehead. He could feel his heart thumping within him as if with a sledge hammer trying to get out. These were signs both his wife and his physician would have seriously chastised him for.

"What the fuck do they expect me to do?" ranted the President, banging his fist on the desk hard enough to cause everything on the desk top to jump and clatter. The phone fell off its cradle. Barker retrieved it. Was the bang of the fist intended to enforce the President's question or to demonstrate his anger? It did not really matter. It did both.

"Can I pluck miracles from the sky? Do they think this is not real – that it'll go away? Those Californian Cretins! If we apply this tax flat rate right across the country as they want me to, all the States and cities that are teetering on the brink of bankruptcy will go under. Look how many cities have filed for bankruptcy already! This'll have 'em lining up at the door! They're on their knees. But these Californians! This lot still want their gas guzzling lives – business as usual. It's not as if they're much better off. California's been in the economic shit for years. But they have the advantage of size. With an economy that big they'll just have to find ways. Heaven forbid we restrict their lifestyles."

The group facing the onslaught was small and select, all close friends of the President – and allies. He had called the meeting in Karl Cheever's office instead of the Oval Room or even in his own study to underline that this was more of a personal get together than an official one. Indeed it was, by far, more than a personal get together. In anyone's language, this was a plea for help. Coming from a President it may not have sounded like one. Presidents do not normally plead for help. But that is what this was.

Within the Vice President's office in which they now stood listening to this tirade was Vice President Cheever himself, a man the President had known since college days. There was the still panting Barker. Others included Secretary of State Bill Masters who was in so many ways in sharp contrast to Barker. A former Marine who maintained his ramrod straight back, he stood more than six feet five inches tall and still retained a shock of thick, wiry, white hair. He had always had white hair and lots of it. It was said that he looked old when he was young and now looked young when he was old. He looked 55 and nothing like his real 73 years.

Finally there was industrialist Max Trueman, a self-made man. Known to be ruthless, he mostly wore a smile to the world each day, whatever the day threw at him, whatever thoughts his brain was generating. He could, it was said of him, place a hangman's noose around a man's neck and still smile at him while doing so! It was assumed to be a metaphoric statement. Nobody had actually seen him do it! Though the ruthlessness was less manifest these days, Trueman could still cut a man down with a lash of the tongue but, as a reflection of his maturity and longevity, would continue to smile gently as he did so.

These were the President's confidants, his 'Knights Templar' as the suspicious media had nicknamed them. "Bullshit," the President frequently responded or with worse expletives on bad days. But there was no denying these were his trusted inner sanctum, his soul mates and blood brothers – his Knights. In his first term of office this group had, in essence, become the power base of his administration - an unconstituted, inner sanctum, policy cabinet. It was a power group the President consistently denied had any power or influence and yet consistently demonstrated it had an abundance of both.

"And what are the Chinese playing at? What the hell's going on? Who is going to help me sort this mess out?" raged the President.

His explosion was the culmination of a series of events in recent history, enough to concern any leader of the USA. Even in a relatively short period of time he had witnessed a seismic shift of global power from West to East. Russia, constantly teetering on the brink of financial meltdown, now held a golden stack of cards in the form of both oil and gas. It was not just the financial value of these resources it enjoyed but the political power that came with it. Russia was now calling the tune in a way Moscow had not seen since the glory days at the height of the old Soviet Union. There were hints of new Soviet imperialistic ambitions.

Now India, with a population four times that of America, was on a massive social restructuring programme, moving millions of people from poor rural areas into rapidly growing, new urban worlds. Its gross use of energy had rocketed and was continuing to do so. In South America, Brazil was emulating the Indian story with other South American states such as Venezuela not so far behind.

This was clearly a global shift of power of massive consequence that was stirring across the planet. But the real new power block was China. Like a super tanker, this gargantuan nation had stormed its way into the upper echelon of global political influence. This enormous country was undergoing a new revolution at breath-taking speed. New cities, new power stations, new pressures on resources were a daily occurrence. This was creating a global stress on the world's limited resources, especially in some vital areas such as energy and precious metals. The Chinese had, for instance, cornered the global supply of rare earth metals, a strategic resource used in a wide variety of applications from military technology to mobile phones. It had had serious implications for many US businesses. The Chinese grip on rare earth metals had seen their commodity price go ballistic, on one occasion trebling in value in just one week.

Across the globe, Chinese influence was escalating, its power and impacts being no better exemplified than where it was buying up swathes of land under which valuable minerals were to be found. In Africa, South America, even places like Australia, the asset growing was at an unprecedented scale and pace and sometimes quite surreptitious or even example of outright clandestine acquisition by stealth. The more suspicious and cynical members of the President's inner sanctum even suspected that China "owned" other countries now, even if it had not declared the fact.

"My bet is," Masters had said recently during a debate on the European Euro crisis and in a manner that those present did not know whether to take seriously or not, "that China now owns Greece, not that anyone else would want it! But it's quite possible - as a tactical, political move - if they have. It may own other countries that have been selling national bonds to keep their economies alive. It's only some elements within Russia and the Chinese who've got the cash wealth today to do that. And someone was vigorously buying national bonds during the Euro crisis. My bet is it's the Chinese. They're cash rich alright. Russia as a state has its own financial worries but it does have cash rich Oligarchs."

The impact of the new, rapidly growing economies and their arrival in the world of consumerism, was sending energy costs rocketing everywhere - at a massive rate. America, as the world's biggest energy user, was beginning to be damaged. Costly energy was a new experience for Americans. They were used to having it cheap and readily available. After all, America was the Mecca of oil exploration and recovery and historically they had developed a culture of energy usage which gave little consideration to its price because, up to now, it had been so readily and cheaply obtainable.

Even the coming of shale oil and gas and its major positive impact on markets, was a slow transition bogged down with political indecision and infighting between political parties and the Senate and the House of Representatives. There were major policy clashes with the President's austerity programme, designed to slash national, state and city budget deficits, crashing now into a new-found confidence based on the breakthrough with shale oil and gas.

Faced with a massive fiscal deficit and growing national debt, the President a year ago formed a consultation panel to consider the problem and make recommendations.

The major outcome from their deliberations was the recommendation to introduce a 'National Fuel Tax Differentiator' into which the President had reluctantly bought. The idea was simple, a new fuel tax, but one to be applied State by State - higher for wealthier States where the consumption of fuel was the greatest, and lower in the poor States where consumption was lower. The methodology meant that it could be claimed, with some justification, not to be just a cash earning tax for the Government but an incentive to push people towards reducing their energy use and their carbon emissions, another national political target.

Realising the magnitude, importance and political sensitivity of this proposed scheme, the President had stepped in and undertaken the launch of the report himself, taking that responsibility away from the Chairman of the consultation panel who had been looking forward to delivering the launch speech. The President had intervened and instigated the change less than an hour before the press conference, deliberately engendering an element of theatrical drama but sending both White House officials and those of the panel into a frenzied panic of confusion and uncertainty.

The response had been explosive. Nobody likes a new tax whatever it is, however it is applied. But another tax on fuel it was. And in the wake of others recently applied, this one was aimed especially at the affluent, high quantity energy users. It produced an especially vitriolic response. At the launch of the report, when the President told the Nation he believed he had no option but to adopt the proposals which he felt to be "fair and equitable" at a time of "global pressures beyond our control", he was booed and jeered.

The media was immediately up in arms against the proposal and the President's standing in the ratings took a dive of unprecedented proportions.

"Unfair" was one of the milder accusations thrown at him. Nowhere was objection sounded louder than in California where the local media more or less asked the question: "how dare the President treat us like this! We are, after all, the world's ninth largest economy. We have annual productivity figures bigger than places like Australia, Canada, Mexico and other apparently affluent nations". But, despite its size, California had been fighting annual budget deficits for some time. So the President's tax, weighted against them but in favour of other states, was seen by many to be a crippling and unfair penalty.

And now, today, had come the news that China had approached the Governor of California and suggested some sort of contra deal between the two – and at that level, not at a bi-national one. The White House had not even been consulted and had had no idea about the scheme until the Washington Post broke it as a front page exclusive that morning. It was not the best start to everyone's day in the White House!

CHINESE OIL FOR CALIFORNIA CHIPS screamed the WP headline.

The verbal explosion when the President saw it and read the story echoed around the White House. Telephone lines become heated as secretaries desperately tried to respond to the President's immediate demand and searched for the members of the 'Knights Templar.' They were perfunctorily summoned to an immediate assembly in the Vice President's office.

"I understand Jack the meeting between Al and the Chinese was arranged through an intermediary," said Barker, "an outfit called Asian Pacific Trading Incorporated."

"Who the hell are they?" snapped the President.

"I've got checks going on right now," responded the media man. "It seems they're a Chinese government procurement agency of sorts – but not mainstream. There seems to be some South Korean influence but we're not sure. We're having some difficulty finding out more about them. But we're working on it."

"God almighty!" blasted the President. "First the fucking Chinese. Now the Koreans. What the hell's going on? Who are these people? Why can't we be certain what we're up against? "

"Well as I hear it," continued Barker "their front of shop is fine. Looks kosher enough but a bit doubtful on the edges. That's why we're taking a closer look."

The President grunted. Barker carried on.

"We believe that a group of Chinese officials - and some Koreans - who we assume came from this APTI outfit - spent a week in California with Al and his mob. And I gather they went to a number of different university establishments while they were there."

"So why weren't we involved?" shouted the President.

"Because we weren't invited," said an increasingly dejected Secretary of State Bill Masters.

"So Al is intent on doing a deal for California and breaking out of the new tax. Is that it?" grunted the President looking around his gathered Knights.

Heads nodded in agreement, perhaps a little reluctantly.

"What the hell has he got that's excited the Chinese so much?" As he spoke the President pulled at his shirt collar to such an extent the button broke from the cotton and pinged its way across the room.

"Shit" said the President looking in the direction the button had flown.

"Advanced nano-technology," replied Max Trueman to the original question.

"What in hell's name is that?" groaned the President.

"Well Jack," replied the industrialist, "some people think it's the world's next quantum leap - another milestone moment. Like the invention of the wheel – penicillin – television – the world-wide web. Things that have taken our so-called civilisation forward in a giant leap. There's a lot of talk about how much we need another new quantum leap to confront the combination of challenges we face – like climate change - population growth - the emergence of these new superpowers like China, India, Brazil which are consuming stuff at such an alarming rate - and which are starting to look like the West in the way they live - so they want more of what we already consume."

"Basically we're heading for a situation where there's just not enough resources to go round. We need some radical solutions to all of this and we need them fast. Maybe that's what a Californian university has found. A radical solution. A quantum leap. And they're willing to trade that for oil."

Trueman paused, took a swig from one of an array of water filled glasses that sat on a silver tray on a side desk. "And lately," he continued, "there's been a lot of talk about nano-technology providing that next quantum step – that next giant leap. Hopefully a leap that'll solve some of these growing problems."

"Like what?" asked the President.

But before the industrialist could answer a phone rang. The Vice President moved swiftly, lifted the phone, dialled a number, and put it down again. It remained silent.

"I don't know enough about it to answer that," continued Trueman. "But I do know that some Californian scientists recently went public with a motor that's hundreds of times smaller than a human hair."

"Really?" said the President. "And though that's fascinating, what's it got to do with what we're talking about? Where are you going with this Jake?"

The industrialist shrugged his shoulders. "Who knows? But if you can make a motor that small - a motor that you could for instance inject into the human blood stream, God knows what else these guys are up to. My bet is that in some lab in California they've hit a quantum leap - and that's the card they're dealing to the Chinese".

"In return for oil," muttered the President.

"So they don't have to pay your taxes," responded the industrialist. "What I don't understand though is how come the Chinese are trading in oil? They haven't got enough to meet their own needs let alone sell it to someone else. They're a net importer of oil. So why sell it? And at a time when their fast growing economy is devouring the stuff."

"God only knows," said the President. "And what's Al up to? Declaring UDI is he? Going on his own and ignoring the centre."

"I don't know what Al's up to any more than you," responded Bill Masters. "But since you won your second term of office you know there's been a resurgence of independence talk across the Southern States. And it's continuing. Look what's happened in Texas with their Texas National Movement and their opinion polls. Not far off 100,000 people signed it. An anti-separation pole only got 3,500 signatures. I know they're not big figures but from small fires do big fires grow. And though I don't think this has got legs in Texas, they've done it before - in 1861 - but it was a very different world then."

"But California's a different ball game. It's certainly big enough to be treated seriously - ninth biggest economy in the world behind Brazil, Italy and the UK. You know it contributes more to central government than it receives - all good stuff to support those who promote independence. And while Texas hasn't got the Governor backing the campaign, California has. It's got Al!"

The President thought about this for a while before looking at his friends and saying in a voice that was barely audible, the words carefully chosen and slowly delivered.

"We've got to nail this critter fast. Cut the bastard before it blooms. This could split the Union. It could be the start of the end of the United States."

Chapter 3

The Flying Bird Tea Shop is not far from the centre of Seoul, the monolithic capital of South Korea with its population of more than 10 million. The internationally renowned tea shop is accessed from a modest entrance leading off a crowded, bustling, narrow main road lined by an almost carnival-like jingle jangle of colourful chaos. Food carts purveying endless varieties of snacks create a kaleidoscope of aromas. Filled with Tteokbokki rice cake stews, sticky bbobki lollies, Odeng fish cakes, Dakkochi grilled chicken skewers, kimbap rolls and other oriental wonders, these gastronomic carts mix with sellers of wood carvings, Chinese lanterns, fans, silk scarves and other nick-knacks aimed at the tourists. It creates a chaos of colours and smells but both locals and tourists alike enjoy the offerings from the food carts which always seem to be doing a roaring trade.

Sum Taeyoung had insisted they met at the Flying Bird Tea Shop in the Insadong neighbourhood. Whenever he was resident in Seoul, Sum routinely drank tea there every afternoon if his busy scheduled permitted. It was his unbending belief that the enormously wide variety of blends served there would ensure his continued good health and long life. So, as routinely as he could, he visited this famous tea shop to sip its different variety of teas. His staple diet was the infamous double harmony tea containing dried roots, ginger, ginseng, cinnamon bark, and other medicinal ingredients. Its aroma, let alone its bitter taste, convinces most people that it has potent powers.

Three men sat in a group in a corner amongst the disorder of dimly lit paper lanterns, shelves of china pottery and odds and ends – and the occasional fluttering bird that, with a flash of startling colours and long trailing feathers, flew by or sometimes landed for an inquisitive look around and a peck at any dropped food bits. The mood throughout the tea room was, as ever, the personification of tranquility thanks to the intoxicating mix of traditional music, the smell of herbal teas, and the exotic, colourful small birds.

But it was not a tranquil trio of men who sat in the corner. There was a discernable tension between them. They had not long arrived. Sum and Chan had walked through the busy market stall streets from the nearby HQ of a company called Sustainable Development Brokers International, a business Sum and others had formed some 10 years before.

Born of a South Korean mother and English father, Sum had been educated in London and New York. Rejecting orthodox career opportunities, Sum had gone straight into testing his entrepreneurial talents with a few skirmishes into business in the UK. This had included experimenting with some very dubious ways of making fast money, an objective Sum saw as a basic raison d'etre for going into business. Whilst some of these ventures proved to be very lucrative and successful, Sum also saw what he considered to be a major, global opportunity which caused him to return to his home country of South Korea to see if he could exploit it. He formed another new company and it quickly became clear that he was right - the circumstances and timing could not have been more opportune.

Called Sustainable Development Brokers International, or SDBI for short, the new venture had been seriously successful from day one, very quickly linking Western expertise to Asian needs as mainly China but other areas of Asia including South Korea launched into massive and fast social transformation and economic development programmes. These included the mass migration of people from rural to urban locations. Many city and town development and expansion activity, driven almost singularly by economic judgements and at huge pace, started to pay a major penalty as urban growth generated more pollution and air quality problems. Water provision too became a major difficulty for many expanded communities and energy needs escalated at unprecedented rates. So the need for 'sustainable' development - in which equal consideration is given to economic, social and environmental targets - increasingly became not only understood but needed, urgently in some cases.

Indeed, the Chinese experience was proving to be a grand example of how not to achieve sustainable development with environmental problems starting to hinder economic growth and cause social distress. The most obvious examples were smog ridden cities and the increasing problem of clean water provision for growing urban communities. Sum spotted this as a major opportunity. SDBI was formed to link Eastern needs to Western knowledge and experience and that formed the front of shop - the highly visible, highly successful image of SDBI.

It had also, as the business progressed, become quite normal for SDBI to spin off subsidiary companies, formed to control and manage specific projects. It was easier that way to segregate and manage money flows and keep project budgets separated. Amongst a host of such spin-offs could be found Asian Pacific Trading Inc though it would take a formidable and determined researcher to find a direct link between APTI and SDBI. To the outside world APTI looked to be of Chinese government origin. Sum had many skills but he was especially clever at weaving corporate structures that could conceal what needed to be concealed. And the link between APTI and SDBI was one such link Sum wanted to remain deeply in the shadows.

Also hidden in the murky corners of the corporate structure and deliberately concealed in a sophisticated and complex cauldron of confusion and behind many, many Chinese walls, lay a darker reason for SDBI's existence. It was this element of the corporation that Sum now concentrated on most though he still remained involved in some of the bona-fide business activity. The dark side of SDBI was a cast back to his early days in business and schemes which he found to be quick money earners, embracing such things as drug trafficking and gun running. This side of the business - whilst very profitable as well as being a fast cash generator - also served to satisfy Sum in other ways. Though educated in the West, Sum had come to despise the basic principles of capitalism and what he considered its imperialistic origins and antecedents - as he saw them to be. He saw what he interpreted to be the parasitical activities of the British Empire which, having militarily overrun underdeveloped countries, then asset stripped them. The French, Portuguese and Spanish were all culpable in history and, more recently, the Americans had become the new imperialistic raper of the world.

On such illicit and immoral activity had modern day industrial societies and capitalism been born. And he could see that its main alternative – communism - as delivered in Russia and before that the Soviet Union and now in China – was flawed too. This was, his research had concluded, been mainly because these Communist states had been hot beds of corruption. In his belief, communism only worked in truly dictatorial states, like North Korea, so had limited application opportunities.

However, it also seemed to Sum, that, at worst, capitalism was a redundant and corrupt concept that had also proved impractical or it was the only game in town worth pursuing but badly in need of a makeover. But, in a world troubled by a wide variety of different challenges, Sum saw another opportunity which would satisfy his beliefs but also his bank balance. The more the world was full of challenges and difficulties, the more chaos reigned around the world, so Sum's darker businesses would succeed. SDBI's darker side was designed specifically to stimulate chaos.

But Sum needed a platform to operate from. That is why he had worked fastidiously to ensure SDBI had a legitimacy and international reputation in brokering contacts between East and West that enabled its clandestine activities to function in a unique way.

As usual, Sum had had some difficulty climbing the creaky, narrow, wooden stairs that turned their way up to the first floor. His significant frame of obese proportions and his flowing, traditional Korean robes were not suited for these stairs or the crowded tea room with its very restricted aisles and little space between the tables. The arrays of ornaments that decorated every shelf and unused corner were a nightmare to circumnavigate in anything other than tight fitting clothes. He puffed and panted his way to the top, a charismatic figure in his flowing garbs made even more flamboyant because of his extravagantly long hair and long beard. If this was a man trying to keep a low profile he seemed to go about it in a very strange way. His very physique and his colourful attire turned heads wherever he went.

"Just tell me what happened and what the current position is," Sum spoke in English but with a soft voice in a mixed Korean Asian and English Oxford accent. And though the voice was gentle, both the way he spoke and the steeliness of his eyes were reminders to anyone who needed reminding that Sum was a man with a reputation that said he had little tolerance for those he considered to be fools. He expected to get what he wanted and it was unusual when he did not.

The two who sat with him, both appreciably younger and fitter than he, also worked for SDBI but were currently seconded to APTI. Jo Summers had flown in to Seoul the night before. An American but of Far East Asia parents, he was ex-military. Born in New York, he had exited the army with a blotted record book and a zealous hate of the American administration, American bureaucracy, American arrogance and Americans in general. Though he had lived in the Bronx most of his life, nowadays he felt more Asian than American and certainly that is the direction in which his allegiances now lay. But he did not like Seoul and visited it as little as he could. Though he was not a man who would normally bother about such things, when in Seoul he always yearned for the greenery of Central Park when he was in this massive city with its 40 million people, concrete and more concrete. When in New York Summers loved to escape to the greenery of Central Park. He had come to be almost infatuated by it. But there was one thing wrong with Central Park. It was full of Americans. But at least it had lots of trees.

Chan Yung, sharp minded, still only in his early twenties, South Korean and an IT wizard, had won a global reputation for some of his post-university hacking exploits and would still probably be spending his life in shady web cafes - or in jail - had not SDBI got to hear about him and plucked him into a world of global adventure and serious rewards.

It was Chan who first responded. "You'll remember that you were insistent that Jake, Jo and myself all understood your plan as we were going to be primarily responsible for its delivery. We all agreed that this was a situation where we needed to meet and talk. Not something to be done remotely or virtually. We were also concerned that anything but a real get together, face to face, would have potential security weaknesses. So we agreed to meet. But trying to get the three of us together was very difficult. Jake's schedule in particular was crazy. The first opportunity was in Scotland. Jo and I were scheduled to go to Germany so we felt we could meet in Scotland where Jake already had three days of meetings on the north coast. You'll remember, Jake was following up your suggestion about technology and experience transfer from the decommissioning of the old nuclear power station at Dounreay."

"I remember," grunted Sum.

Chan waited momentarily to see if Sum was going to say more. But he did not. So Chan continued.

"I know Jake will report to you and may have done so already but the discussions he was having were complex and involved not just Dounreay Site Restoration Limited but representatives of the companies that own DSRL. The job there is massive. Jake told us that there's lots of vested interests so it made his discussions about an agency arrangement for SDBI very difficult. He told us about one example of the complexity of the decommissioning task there. There's this pit. It had radioactive waste thrown into it for nearly 20 years until there was an explosion in 1977 and they stopped the practice. According to Jake, the clean-up of the pit has got to be done by an enormous robotic crane. It's going to cost £4 million just to clean the pit up."

Chan paused in anticipation of another comment from Sum. But none was forthcoming so he went on with his report.

"We particularly wanted to talk about the chess code you'd laid out for our project. I'd written up a synopsis of both the project and the chess idea but to ensure its security I'd encrypted it all into a QR code which I put onto an APTI letterhead and aligned it to my iPhone. The only way you could read it was via my own iPhone and maybe link that to an iPad or similar."

"What's a QR code?" asked Sum quietly. He knew little about new technologies. He left such things to people like Chan.

"It's short for Quick Response. They're like small printed icons that can hold vast amounts of information. You must have seen some. They look like a very small square that has a pattern - a bit like a maze. You can scan a QR or use your iPhone to photo it and the information then becomes available. But we had tinkered with this QR so only my phone could read it. I'd sent it to Jake but without my phone he couldn't read it. I sent it to him anyway to show what we were doing."

Chan paused. Yet again there were no more questions. He continued.

"So Jo and I hired a Gulfstream to take us from New York to Aberdeen and then on to Germany. We refuelled at Prestwick on the West side of Scotland and eventually landed at the nearest available airport to the north coast of Scotland - at Wick."

"I'd hoped we could have flown straight into Dounreay. There used to be a big runway there. We now know it started life as a World War two airfield but it's not been used for aircraft for years. They use it as a car park now for all the people working on the decommissioning of the atomic plant. So we had to go to Wick and then drive up to a motel on the outskirts of the nearest town to Dounreay - Thurso."

"Jake was staying at the motel but he said he didn't want to meet us there."

"He was pretty awkward about it all," interjected Summers.

"No," responded Chan. "He didn't like the idea of meeting in the motel. He thought it would be too busy. Too many people who might be curious. Perhaps people who he knew through the meetings he'd already had at the power station. So he suggested we meet at this inn. I've no idea how he knew about the inn. Maybe he saw it on a map. I don't know. I never asked him."

"All a bit crazy," interrupted Summers sweeping a landing bird off the table with the back of his hand. "The man's paranoid. We'd have been better off and less conspicuous in a crowd."

"So we used the hire car to drive to the inn," continued Chan. "It was in the middle of nowhere and hardly anyone in it when we got there - just the innkeeper, a local and some dude working on a laptop by the open fire. He didn't look like a local but the others seemed to know him well enough."

"We found a table as far away from everyone else as we could - which wasn't that far because the place was tiny."

"It was a bum idea," interrupted the American again, repeating the point he'd made earlier. "It's better to get lost in a crowd rather than hide away from everyone. I felt uneasy about it from the start. A bum idea. But Jake held the cards. We were jumping to his tune."

Chan paused for some intake of tea before continuing. "Jake arrived about ten minutes later. He looked really out of place with his slick Singapore city suit and briefcase."

"Bum idea," muttered Summers. "Might as well have had a neon light on him the way he looked. But we all attracted attention. Couldn't do otherwise. A real bum idea."

Chan frowned at Summers. The continuous interruptions were unnerving him and upsetting the way he was trying to tell his story. But he continued.

"So we held this muttered meeting. I don't think anyone would have heard anything. Though the room was quite small, the people at the bar were too far away to overhear us and the guy with the laptop had a pair of headphones on and I could hear the jazz he was playing while he worked. He wouldn't have heard us."

"Anyway, we talked about the project and I guess we were together for about an hour and a half."

"Jake gave us an update on how the Chinese were responding and he said that the most important thing now was to get California to sign up to an agreement in principle before we got into more detail. Back in the US I had prepared two of our letterheads with the QR in it. Jake had got the one I had sent him and I had another copy. In the inn, I scanned the QR with my phone so we were able to read it and talk about it. It wasn't easy doing it that way. Reading the document off the phone and talking about it was awkward but it was the safest way to do it. Anyway, the point is there were two letterheads with us that had the QR on them."

"We were just clearing up and getting ready to leave the place when the only other person to enter the inn all evening - the wife of the proprietor - came in. Outside a storm had got up and when the outside door opened our papers flew everywhere. So did the papers of the guy by the fire and there was several moments of chaos as we gathered everything up and worked out what belonged to who. I saw that Jo had got our papers. I saw him put them inside his case."

"After we'd cleared up we left - went back to Thurso. We stayed overnight and headed back to Wick the next day and on to Germany."

"It was two days later, after we had done Berlin and we're well on the way back to the States, when Jake dropped the bombshell. He had a growing suspicion which he had to check out with us."

"He spoke to Jo."

"He asked if we'd got a copy of the letterhead we'd looked at at the inn. I said no. I thought he'd got them both. He said was I sure? I said yes. I'd seen him pick them up after the meeting and put them in his case. But Jake told me he had only picked up one copy. He eventually had this growing unease and felt he needed to check I had picked one of them up. But I hadn't. If I hadn't got one, one was missing."

There was a long silence. Around them other visitors to the tea shop chatted away their voices mixing with the almost inaudible tinkling musical sounds of the shop. They supped their exotic teas. The small, colourful birds flew in their chaotic way and the slow pace of the tea experience clashed with the tension now surrounding the three men at the corner table.

"So what have you done about this?" asked Sum, head bowed so the other two could not see his face and the scowl of anger now upon it.

Chan and Summers told him. They spelt it out in every detail they could think of. Anything to reassure the big South Korean. And they spoke with the levels of anxiety and conviction of men who were fighting for their lives. For that, they both knew, was exactly what they were now doing.

"From the US," said Summers, bent towards Sum so he could keep his voice low but to ensure the big man heard every word, "we made contact with a cleanup team we've used many times before. They're Eastern European but based in Brussels. They went up to the inn, got there in two days by motorbike. There were three people in the place when they arrived and they took them out. We had told them to do that so if anyone had any knowledge about anything they wouldn't be able to talk about it. Seemed like overkill - but appropriate. They searched the place from top to bottom but found nothing."

Chan took up the account. "The three people were the inn proprietor and his wife and a local. But we had remembered the guy with the laptop and the papers. The guy whose papers had got mixed with ours when the wind blew everything everywhere. He wasn't there when the cleanup team went in."

There was a pause as Chan and Summers looked at each other to see who would continue. But before they could speak Sum did. "Who is this fourth person?" the question was so soft it could almost not be heard.

Summers hesitated. Chan replied.

"We don't know," he admitted with a distinct tremor in his voice. "But we have left mechanisms in place to find out."

There was a long silence before the large man with the avalanche of hair said in a hardly audible Asian/Oxford voice: "I hope your mechanisms are effective. And quick. I have invested considerable time and money in this project. Nobody will compromise it. Nobody will screw it up. Understand?" Chan and Jo both nodded. They certainly understood.

Chapter 4

"I was expecting a woman," the fresh faced young PC said to Bond who sighed wearily. How many times had he heard this? He could have killed his dad and his warped sense of humour! It was also Ian Fleming's fault! The author had chosen their family surname for his internationally renowned fictitious spy hero, But it was his dad who had compounded the problem by insisting his son had this Christian name that sounded feminine. But he had and Gene Bond had had to live with the consequences all his life. He should, he thought for perhaps the thousandth time, have changed it. But, somehow, he had never got round to it. Now, at his maturing time of life, it was probably too late.

"No, it's Gene with a G not a J," he responded with some frustration. "My dad was a Johnny Cash fan. You know - 'My name's Sue - how do you do'. The famous concert at Folsom Prison in California?"

The young officer nodded but the blank expression showed he obviously had no idea what the man standing in front of him was talking about. Bond realised the years between them were too great. Johnny Cash meant nothing to this young lad in uniform. So, dismissing the subject as if it didn't matter any more, the young policeman sought to keep his mind on the task before him. This incident was something way beyond his experience or comfort zone.

Earlier Bond had thrived on the drive to the inn. In his younger years, before even reaching the age of 10, he had become a map freak. He was infatuated by them. Before his age reached double figures he was drawing his own 'pretend maps' complete with contour lines. He used them to play battle games. As the years moved on he took to delving into Ordnance Survey maps. They fascinated him. And every time he looked at the map of the very north of the United Kingdom there was this Aroad - the A836. It wound its way from the East to West right across the top of the country. He became enthralled by the idea of one day driving its full length. There was a certain unfathomable, irrational, hard to explain romance to the notion. Now, all these years later, Bond knew virtually every inch of the road by heart.

He had been on a business trip to Aberdeen when his love affair with this part of the country started. He had taken time off to explore an area of the UK he had never seen before and happened to find himself driving north through the Caithness Flowlands, a spectacular area of rare tundra with huge valleys bordered by massive mountains but with the valley beds a patchwork of rough land and lochs, some small, some big. It was a land of deer, buzzards, sometimes even a high flying eagle – and of sheep – everywhere. He found it breathtaking.

But further north there was more surprise - enormous sandy beaches, mostly devoid of people even in the best of weather, and wonderful views out to sea. In some areas there were small islands off the mainland while on the horizon the clear view of nothing but sea was interrupted to the East by the black silhouette of the Orkney Isles. He walked coastal tracks - sheep and deer tracks - and while the views were always outstanding, whatever the weather, on warm and sunny days in summer the smell of the heather, mixing with orchids and the salty air of the sea, was intoxicating.

Bond loved it and returned several times before stumbling across a derelict crofter's cottage that was for sale. It was too good to miss and he bought it as a retreat from his mainly city life and the suffocating world of commercialism.

Tonight was a classic Scottish North Coast night. The moon was big, vivid and seemingly bursting with glow in a sky full of bright stars. Thick black clouds scuttled at speed across the coast, heading inland from the cold expanses of the North Sea, some dropping heavy loads of water as they made land. Naked of clouds, the moon and a heaven of stars gave off so much light the world looked like a monochrome version of day time. It was bright enough to cast shadows. But when a fast travelling cloud crossed the path of the moon this strange, almost half daylight was plunged into an inky blackness.

The northerly wind was gusting strongly, buffeting the Porsche. The bleaker and darker moments of the journey were frequently accompanied by torrents of driving rain. This was not the weather for the fainthearted. As he fought for visibility, Bond thought this was more a night to batten down the hatches, to stoke up the peat fire, to reach for the whisky bottle, and to share an intimate interlude with wife, girlfriend or mistress. Currently Bond had none of these. Life was too busy, too dominated by his business which in turn was dominated by his passion - the values of sustainable development.

The Porsche grumbled and growled as he made his way West. The exhaust crackled and popped angrily as he used gears, engine and brakes to fast lose speed as the car entered an upward climbing hairpin bend. Bond worked hard to keep the car on the optimum line. The headlights cut and arced through the darkness, lighting up scrubland and - inevitably - a few sheep before sweeping round to illuminate the road again. Occasionally he caught sight of the sea to his right. It was an extraordinary shimmering metallic colour when the moon was on it. He had glimpses of great cliff edges darkly silhouetted in the night light, brief and teasing views of white surf creaming up vast beaches and, sometimes, in the near distance, high, white-topped mountains, black and solid monoliths.

He loved driving this road. It fulfilled all the romance he had anticipated in his youth. He was mortified when the original single track road was replaced by a modern highway. He expected his driving delight and challenge to be wrecked by the arrival of this new ultra-smooth, twin lane stretch of tarmac. But one fun challenge was replaced by another. He was amazed that modern day engineering could produce such a road with occasional negative cambered bends and tightening curves, unexpected encounters that sometimes took high flying continental motorcyclists - riding too fast for the testing conditions - skidding off into the wild countryside either side.

But he knew every inch of the road - and used it to his advantage as he pushed the Porsche close to its limits of adhesion. The only unknown factor to Bond was that unpredictable hazard of the north - sheep. But this evening even they seemed to be behaving themselves, mostly lying to the side of the road, protecting themselves in the ditches from the bitterly cold wind, chewing as ever and giving the Porsche a bored look as it flew by. He was 20 minutes from the inn when he encountered the only vehicle he was to see in the whole 40 mile drive - a motorcycle heading East with a rider and passenger.

He enjoyed the drive - and he was full of expectation for the meeting that was taking him to the inn. There he would delight in the company of Jimmie Mackay whose companionship he relished and whose friendship he truly loved. It remained an astonishment to him that the two had become such close friends – a largely city dwelling, middle aged Englishman and an old, wizened northern Scottish crofter who epitomized the characteristics of a rugged and somewhat battered feudal farmer. The two had struck a friendship that had now lasted nearly 20 years. Together they downed copious amounts of whisky and philosophised about great and worldly matters. They met both in the local inn and at Jimmie's nearby crofter's cottage. If the meeting was in the latter, whatever time of day, Jimmie would pour a good half tumbler of the gold liquid, often out of an unmarked bottle. Bond had never had the courage to ask its origins. He took it to be the North Scotland equivalent of Moonshine. It tasted gorgeous, soft and peaty, and had a prodigious alcoholic kick.

They both shared interest in politics. Bond was astonished how well-read Jimmie was with a wide knowledge, especially of both Scottish and English history. He had a memory that defied his years. In the early days of their relationship Bond could hardly understand what the aged crofter was saying. On average, he reckoned to pick up about two or three words a sentence, so strong was Jimmie's Scottish accent, an interpretation of English that owed much to his Gaelic origins. When Jimmie forgot to put his false teeth in - not a rare incident - this average success per sentence plummeted to near zero! But over the years the level of understanding had increased and a union beyond that of friendship had grown between the two men.

Jimmie was an integral and central part of a Bond business plot. Bond loved projects. Projects made things happen, could often find funding, and had tangible, measurable outputs. And the project he and Jimmie were working on fulfilled many of Bond's objectives. It had fallen as if from the skies during one of the whisky driven philosophical debates.

"Och, I dunna understand what you're aboot," Jimmie had said. Bond had been talking about how "we humans are seriously damaging the planet and we're killing off many other species that we share the planet with. What right have we to do that? And we're using resources at a greater rate than they're available, we're polluting the atmosphere, we're discarding waste in disgraceful volumes and, apart from anything else, causing havoc at sea with marine life. The chances are we're causing climate change and encouraging more extremes of weather. We're causing social unrest though lack of equitable distribution of wealth and showing little or no real concern for those who struggle to survive."

Bond had deliberately tried to keep away from the jargon that so often dominated his professional life. So he was amazed at Jimmie's response.

"Och, you know about The Clearances. I know. We've talked about them enough."

Indeed they had. This proud North Scottish crofter was all too pleased to be able to recount that he was related to those who had been the victims of the notorious Highland Clearances.

"Those responsible - those Scottish gentry who had seen how their English counterparts in Westminster were making fortunes from sheep, determined to do the same by turning their land over to sheep too. But to satisfy their greedy ambitions they had to clear the land of people who had lived on it for generations. They considered those people - my antecedents - to be vagabonds and vagrants - worthless gypsies. But I tell you Bond, those people survived off their own skills. They tended their land and grew their own tatties and neeps. They reared their own animals as feed for themselves. They built their own homes. They made their own clothes. Damn it man, they even mined their own minerals and made their own pots and pans. They were - by anyone's standards - sustainable communities."

Bond was amazed and deeply impressed that his aged Scottish crofting friend had used the word 'sustainable'. Sustainable development was what dominated Bond's life but rarely did he find people who truly understood what it meant. He thought it extraordinary that he had had to come to the very top of the UK and deep into the Scottish feudal crofting community to find someone who understood quite fundamentally what it was about.

It had drawn the two of them even closer together. It made Bond think that maybe the world was going round in some sort of progressive circle - sort of back to the future - and that modern day life had much to learn from people like the crofters and those who preceded them from before the days of the Clearances. Maybe communities that were self-contained within feudal systems such as theirs were the epitome of the sustainable development model he preached.

From that had grown 'the project'. It was Bond's idea but one Jimmie supported though his cynical nature had ensured they tested the idea to exhaustion before the crofter agreed to be involved. Bond was greatly concerned about promoting any project in this northerly part of Scotland. He needed Jimmie to be part of it. Any idea seen to be conceived and promoted by an 'outsider' - and, perhaps, especially an Englisher, was likely to antagonize the locals and be ridiculed. The idea had grown from a question Bond had asked of Jimmie.

"Why is it Jimmie, if I go into a supermarket in Thurso or Wick I can buy New Zealand lamb but I can't buy lamb labelled Caithness or Sutherland lamb or even Northern Scottish lamb? The environmental consequences of transporting lamb here from what must be the farthest point on the planet away from Northern Scotland must be staggering. And it's so ironic because you can't drive down a road here without the potential of hitting a sheep. It seems plain daft to me!"

And the two had gone on to debate the question. Bond eventually said: "What we need to do is to bring the crofters together so their collective numbers of sheep add up to the sort of volumes the supermarkets talk about. The supermarkets want secure supply chains. The public increasingly wants traceable meat. Together, working in some sort of collective way, you crofters could provide that."

"Och Gene", responded Jimmie. "What you mean is a Kibbutz."

Bond was amazed. "Bloody hell! What do you know about Kibbutz?" he responded.

"You forget Gene, I fought in Palestine for the British Army. I fought alongside Geordies, Scousers, Brummies. A grand gang of men. And we fought amongst the villages, the Kibbutz of the areas. They were self-contained communities, much like the ones cleared in the Scottish Highlands for sheep so the gentry could make their dirty money."

"You're right," Bond had agreed. "We need to bring the crofters together. Surely we could do that? They could even establish their own abattoir to process their own meat. The market has never been keener for traceable food produce than now. We should be able to offer lamb where the consumer can go as far as tracing which croft the animal was reared on, when it was born, what protective treatments it's received - and so on. 'North Scottish Lamb' could become a really strong brand."

And once they had started down that route more opportunities had emerged including the potential of crofters jointly owning wind turbines in ventures with the companies that would supply and install the machinery and link it to the national grid, but who would share the generated income with the local crofting community. Bond pointed out how similar schemes worked elsewhere, giving the local population great benefits.

Inevitably ideas that seemed so sensible, logical and easily delivered when considered over several whiskies, became somewhat different in the cold light of the following morning and in the real world where dreams so regularly flounder. In the real world a myriad of vested interests, jealousies, complex land ownerships and other hurdles often suffocated creative thinking. The crofting laws and the crofters' relationships with the landowners made issues that seemed simplicity itself become complex, bureaucratic and unbelievably frustrating.

So Bond drove on with enthused expectation for the meeting with Jimmie, even though trying to make things happen was full of frustrations and hurdles. The whisky would be good and so would the companionship. It would be, as Jimmie would put it - "a good crack."

As he arrived at the inn it had an even more lonely, cold and dark appearance than usual. There was an unwelcoming feel about it and that was most unusual. He drove onto the rough cut car park to the accompaniment of scrubbing tyres and flying stones. He could not immediately fathom his discomfort but soon realised no other vehicle was to be seen and, very surprisingly, no lights at all shone from the building. The absence of another car was not necessarily that strange at this time of year but the lack of light illuminating the car park and the front of the inn was, in Bond's experience, unheard of. Even out of the tourist seasons, the landlord normally kept the bar open and car park light on in the optimistic anticipation of capturing what little passing trade there might be. Bond hoped he would still be able to get a drink having driven all this way.

With a clear patch of sky providing him with light enough to guide him across the rough surfaced car park, but blasted now and then by powerful gusts of chilling wind screaming in from the sea, Bond walked across to the bar door. He caught hold of the catch, dropped it and pushed. There was no resistance. He had expected none. The door swung open as usual and, also as usual, bashed against the wall. But instead of the customary greeting of warm lights and a cheering fire in the fireplace, Bond was confronted by a wall of darkness. He could see absolutely nothing except a small glow from the embers of a dying fire.

"Hello," he called out. There was no response. He tried again but still did not get a reply. With curiosity increasing and mixing with an equal amount of growing anxiety he felt around for a light switch. Eventually his efforts paid off and he clicked the switch his hand had encountered. The bar lights flickered into life to reveal a scene of carnage - something that the opening curtain of a play might have revealed - or a scene from a TV cops programme. But this was real. Too real. Three bodies lay before him with blood pools alongside each one. Instantly he knew who all three were. And to his horror one was Jimmie. Dear Jimmie - who had survived so much in life and was now lying in a pool of his own blood.

Bond stood there for some time in stone cold horror and disbelief. He could see what he could see but he could not comprehend it. It could not be real. He sensed a gathering of nausea within him and thought he might be sick. His legs felt weak. His heart pounded. He must have stood there a full two minutes before his brain started to function again and he realised he must do something.

His frozen state was eventually replaced with the explosive thought that the perpetrator of this butchery might still be nearby. Bond was shocked and frightened by the thought but soon concluded that any such person would have heard him arrive, heard the door crash open and heard him call out. Surely such a person would have responded already? Not totally convinced, he stepped as quietly as he could back outside and was thankful his mobile phone had a signal. It was not always so in this part of the world. He dialed 999.

It was difficult to relay the story. It sounded preposterous, so incredulous. And again, so annoyingly, his name didn't help. The police phone operator obviously had some difficulty in accepting this wasn't some ridiculous hoax but eventually Bond's persistence won her over.

"There are people on the way to you now," she said. "Do not touch a thing. And please don't go back inside the inn."

Bond did not need the suggestion. He got his flying jacket from the car and strode around the near total darkness of the car park, virtually oblivious to the gusting, cuttingly cold wind but now certain he was alone. Eventually, in the distance, he heard a siren and a blue flashing light came into view.

The law, when it arrived in its slightly dented Ford, was not a local. Bond would have recognised anyone in uniform from the North Coast. This one, he thought, looked young enough to have just escaped the afternoon school class but, nevertheless, was a fully grown policeman. A fledgling PC. He nodded at Bond and commented on the Christian name. He failed to understand Bond's father's poor joke link to the historic rock and roller, a poor joke that Bond would have to live with for ever.

"I'm the first one here then." Bond wasn't sure if it was a question or a statement. It was, he felt, such a ridiculous comment it did not justify a response.

"Is that where the action is?" asked the young officer, nodding in the direction of the front door of the inn.

"Sure is," Bond replied, turning up the collar of his jacket as a squall of thin but penetrating rain heralded the arrival of some more wet weather. "It's like a blood bath in there. A massacre. I've never seen anything like it."

The young policeman walked towards the inn door. "You'd better stay there sir."

"I can tell you who they are," responded Bond not waiting for a reply but now also heading for the door. "And anyway, there's another rain storm about to hit us."

The two walked into the bar, still illuminated from Bond's previous brief visit. The policeman walked slowly and cautiously to the bar, avoiding the corpse of the ancient local, and looked over.

"Shit," he said. "You're right about carnage. Looks like a battlefield. Who are they?"

"You're not from around here are you?" asked Bond.

"No," replied the uniformed youngster. "I'm doing a stint up here from Inverness. So I don't really know anyone around here."

Bond named the victims. "Harry and Barbara Arrowsmith. They run the place. And the old timer there is - or was - Jimmie. A great friend of mine. That's why I was coming here. To see Jimmie. God, I don't believe this has happened! Poor Jimmie."

"What a bleeding mess," the youngster said, blatantly with no idea what to do. His words were badly chosen - but for now forgivable. But he did the sensible thing - and did nothing. Instead they eventually found chairs and sat to wait the arrival of higher authority.

When it came - half an hour later - higher authority was represented by two tall and well worn, mature coppers. One quickly demonstrated his superior status by giving the other and the youngster a series of instructions. Clearly a policeman of experience, his words were quiet and his instructions authoritative.

"And who, sir, are you?" he asked of Bond who managed to reply without the discussion degenerating into the fictitious world of spies, agents and fast cars and women.

"And where do you live?"

Bond told the senior officer he spent much time on the north coast in the regenerated crofter's cottage he had acquired some 20 years before but still maintained a home in the English Midlands.

"And what line of business are you in?"

It was a question Bond always dreaded. It always demanded further explanation, whatever he said, "I'm an environmental entrepreneur," Bond told the officer, giving his standard answer and knowing full well what would come next.

"What on earth does that mean?" asked the policeman. "It sounds a bit grandiose and complicated if you don't mind me saying sir. Can you put it into words I'll understand? And what brought you to this place?"

"Answering your first question first," Bond responded "I try and make money helping businesses make money by helping them save the planet - through things like waste management and renewable energy - but much more as well. And I often come here. Sometimes twice a week when I'm on the North Coast. I like its remoteness. I like the beer. I used to like Harry. And I used to drink with my friend Jimmie. Shit! I can't get over it. Why the hell has this happened? Why here?"

"Why indeed, sir?" pondered the policeman. "The same questions I have. Have you any ideas? If you know them well, have they said anything that might link to this? Has anything unusual happened that you can think of?"

Bond thought a while. An idea came to his mind but he considered it for a while before answering.

"There was an unusual sort of an incident last week. Nothing threatening. Nothing sinister. Just unusual."

And what was that sir?" asked the policeman.

And Bond relayed the story of being in the inn, working on some reports on his laptop when the inn door had been pushed open to allow someone to enter. Both his papers and those of a group of three men on the opposite side of the bar had been blown all over the floor.

"It was all a bit chaotic for a while and the three guys were scrambling around to make sure they got all their papers back. They were obviously concerned they retrieved everything - and they also seemed worried that I might see anything I shouldn't."

"Who were they?"

"I don't know," replied Bond. "I've no idea. Never seen them before or since. They didn't say much and they left soon after getting everything back in order. They were clearly business people – all in suits. Expensive suits at that. They all had a distinct Far Eastern look but I think one – or maybe two - were American."

"You didn't hear what they were talking about?"

"No. When I was working I had my earphones on. I was listening to some jazz. Have no idea what they were on about. And they hardly said anything as they gathered their papers up. Picked them all up, didn't even finish their drinks and went."

The Detective Sergeant looked at Bond long and hard. He passed Bond a business card and said: "if you think of anything else Mr Bond, you phone me at the number on this card. I don't mind what it is and it may be stuff you think isn't important. I'll be the judge of that. So - anything. You phone me. OK? We will undoubtedly want to talk to you again. In the meantime, I suggest you go home now. Keep an eye open and be extremely wary. The people who did this are clearly very, very dangerous. And please don't leave the area without letting me know first."

And Bond left. Puzzled. Worried. A bit sick still. And the drive to the cottage was without the exuberance of the drive West.

Soon the jungle drums of the north coast started to beat. Nothing is really secret in close-knit rural communities like this and when the young policeman told his wife what he had seen and what had happened, so the news passed on. Eventually it reached the ears of a young Thurso girl named Marie who worked on the petrol pumps at the service station overlooking the port of Scrabster, not far from the hotel above the port and on the outskirts of Thurso. She received the news with a tingle of excitement, anticipation, confusion and guilt. But the guilt was outweighed by the promise of reward and she found the piece of paper the stranger with the American accent had left with her and the text number he had scrawled. She got her mobile phone out and sent a text message.

"I think I've found your fourth person. What do you want me to do now?"

Chapter 5

"This is how we hope to save the world's energy crisis".

Brian Kemp held high a small glass laboratory phial so everyone gathered in the small room could see. Inside, an almost opaque and colourless liquid, filled three quarters of the container. From anyone else the claim would have sounded preposterous. But Brian Kemp is a man who just has to be taken seriously. And though this introduction to his most ambitious project to date was a revelation to his visitors, Kemp still had another surprise in store for them.

The English county of Warwickshire is renowned not only for being 'Shakespeare's country' but for its leafy lanes, a reminder that in ancient times much of this central area of England was covered by the Forest of Arden. The group assembled with Kemp stood in the small reception area of his two-farm business. It also doubles up as a small meeting room.

Kemp's farms typify those of the area. They cover several acres of rolling, rich green countryside and are well populated by an array of different trees and thick hedges. Not that either of them knew it, it is located not a great distance from Bond's Midland home.

This group was pleased to have survived the tour of Kemp's estate. It was hard work. Trying to keep up with the 81 year old farmer and energy expert was a tough proposition. Despite his years, Kemp's unbounded enthusiasm for his subject seemed to generate unlimited energy within him and his tours of the various methods he has for generating electric power, scattered as they are across the two farms, was this time, as ever, conducted at an ultra-fast pace. So by the time the group arrived back at the office/meeting room from where the tour had started they were hot and exhausted.

Kemp is in his element when, with great enthusiasm and gusto, he shows his inquisitive guests how he uniquely runs his business. With long white hair, upright stance and long stride, he gives lie to his age. He still, as often as not, works a 16 hour day. His enthusiasm and energy are infectious and seem to function equally wherever he happens to be - on his Warwickshire farms or anywhere around the planet because, despite his age, Brian is still a globetrotter.

Yet to be revealed to this group, because he always kept his biggest secret to last, was the means by which he does much of his travelling.

This man could easily be taken as an eccentric. But he is far from being so. Success has followed him and his family for a long time and Brian is now a man with considerable financial substance. His career has spanned industry and commerce, mostly at command level. Today he has Professor status at three UK universities and two in the USA. He is a special patron to two of these, one in the UK's Midlands and one in California. He has invested many millions of pounds in both and has faculties developed from this finance and which work closely to his own agendas.

A passionate renewable energy man, Brian's never-ending delight is to show people how he runs his business as a totally self-contained energy entity. He has no call at all on external sources of power. He has created it all himself. And when people telephone him, or send him e-mails asking if they can come and see how he has done such a thing, if he is available he will willingly oblige.

This tour, like all the others, started with a presentation in the office/meeting room in which Brian explained why he is so passionate about energy. In his view it is simple. Growing numbers of people on the planet are demanding increasing amounts of energy from a world the resources of which have a distinct limit beyond which we have already passed.

"There were 2.2 billion people on this planet when I was born," he told them. "By the time I die, there'll be close on nine billion. The planet has never seen such escalation in population - never had so many people to cope with - never had so many people yearning for more and more energy."

"So, before we reach breaking point - before we get power blackouts, I decided not to rely on anyone else for my energy. So here we are – completely self sufficient."

And he showed them in pictures what they would see on the tour. There is a lot to see. Brian has got it all! There are the obvious sources of energy the visitors see as they arrive at the farm - the two large wind turbines. Equally evident are the photovoltaic panels - solar panels - seemingly across virtually every roof. Then there is the way farm waste is collected and turned into energy via an anaerobic digestive system. There is the geothermal system that collects energy from deep beneath the farm - and Brian's own hydroelectric scheme - a micro-hydro generator in the fast flowing stream that cuts across his farmland.

And, as if all that is not clever enough, visitors are amazed to find that all these separate devices are computer linked so if one system slows down the dependency for power shifts to others. Excess energy is converted into hydrogen and stored in - of all things - WW2 gas bottles.

"Containing the hydrogen was a major challenge. It took us ages to solve it. But these oxygen bottles really serve the purpose because they were built as strong pressure vessels."

It certainly looks the complex system it is but not necessarily a technologically sophisticated one. Some aspects, especially the oxygen bottles, look perhaps a bit amateurish and cottage industry but it has been checked and approved by the authorities. Indeed, so far advanced are Brian's methodologies they have partly been used to set new UK standards.

The whole scheme has been running for some years, with refinements coming along every now and then. Educated and trained as a scientist, Brian's meticulous approach means he knows exactly what it costs to run his generating scheme and, in terms of capital costs, those had been paid back some time ago. This is a proven, self-contained, virtually no running cost, energy providing system. If anyone doubts that ingenuity and determination cannot win the day, here is living proof that it can. A lot of people talk about 'renewable energy' and 'off-grid systems' and 'decentralised energy'. Indeed, one of Brian's frustrations is the amount of talk and the lack of real action. Here he provides living proof and physical evidence that it can be done.

One of two 'crescendo moments' of the tour comes when Brian talks about his work to produce a new fuel. By now most visitors have got to the stage where they believe this man's ingenuity can achieve anything but a claim of this magnitude stretches incredulity to most people's limits.

Breathless from the high speed tour, this latest group assembled around Brian to hear about his current obsession. "We can take CO2 from air and hydrogen can also come from the air" he tells them. "Consequently it's available in unlimited quantities to everybody. No monopoly. Air goes in and Gasoline comes out - which is carbon neutral."

"We can make as much of this stuff as we like but only in laboratory quantities so far," Brian told them, holding up the small laboratory phial. "We know the principles work. It's based on removing carbon dioxide from air then mixing it with hydrogen. If we can extrapolate that production and take it up to say 30,000 barrels a day, we have basically cracked the world's current energy problem. That's my final challenge. To give the global community the solution."

This seemingly incredulous revelation always generates many questions. But even the most hardened cynic cannot help but be impressed by Brian's knowledge and understanding, backed as it is by the work of laboratories in two of the universities he financially supports.

"So we're looking to build a manufacturing facility to see if we can make the stuff at that sort of volume. That takes investment beyond anything we can do by ourselves so we're still working on that at the moment. And there are other issues too about the way in which you would use the fuel and how it's housed or contained - and we are working on that as well. With any luck we'll have cracked it in, say, five years."

The second 'crescendo moment' was always only revealed right at the end. Leaving the offices again, the visiting party walked away from the farm and towards an eight sided building that is located in the corner of one of his fields. Approaching from the front of the windowless building, a wide concrete drive - rather pointlessly it would seem - leads away from it then stops dead after about 200 yards. The group followed Brian round the back where he opened a small rear door. He stretched out to touch a button to start something that looked as if it had come from Star Wars or International Rescue.

With a buzz and hum of electric motors coming to life, lights flicker into full power to illuminate the inside of the sizeable building. Simultaneously, large doors on the opposite side start to slide open. But what amazes the visitors is the centre piece to the whole drama. Sitting on a sledge-like device that is already moving towards the opening doors is a large, twin engine, jet powered helicopter.

A pilot since his days with the Royal Navy Fleet Air Arm, Brian has been a helicopter pilot ever since and still flies substantial journeys. It enables him to keep close contact with people and projects such as one in the remote Shetland Isles off the north coast of Scotland where local people have built their own wind turbine and converted surplus power into hydrogen, much as Brian has done on his farm. The two projects had for some years collaborated and swapped information and experience as they both developed their ideas and delivered them into practical solutions.

Slightly uncomfortable about accusations of hypocrisy because of the carbon emissions from the helicopter, Brian offsets them by investing in other carbon negative schemes though his friends and staff all argue that he does enough good deeds for that not to be necessary. But Brian does it anyway.

This particular tour was nearly at its end when a member of Brian's team came running down from the office, mobile phone in hand.

"It's a call from the States, Brian. They say it can't wait," said the new arrival.

Brian tutted, annoyed at the interruption. He excused himself from the party by saying farewell and left them to be escorted away by the member of the team who had just arrived. He returned to the office to continue the call.

"We have a growing problem here," said the voice at the other end of the call, a man with an unmistakable American accent who Brian immediately recognised as his permanent staff man in the States. "The Governor is adamant that because the campus is state owned, the state has options on outputs from the institutions. I have gone over and over with him and his team about the question of IP but he says the situation is of such intense value to California the questions of who owns what are irrelevant, including the intellectual property."

"Intellectual property is hardly an irrelevant matter," responded Brian.

"Of course I've told him that," responded the caller. "But he's offering a complex argument about open source information negating the power of IP. He says because you're doing what you're doing and the way you're doing it, IP is irrelevant. You can't have your cake and eat it."

"Have you told him we don't want his money - don't want to sell anything to anyone?" asked Brian. It had always been his plan that if this venture came to anything - if it did provide an answer to the world's energy challenges - he would donate it to mankind in much the same way as Tim Berners-Lee 'gave' mankind the World Wide Web.

"I told him that," said the caller. "But he's being very forceful and of course the University is smelling money. There is some sort of link between the Governor and the Chinese. He's on some sort of deal that has him very excited and very committed."

"He can't force us to do anything," said Brian.

"Well, |I'm not too sure about that," came the anguished reply. "Normally I'd agree. But not in the current climate over here. The Governor is in no mood to argue. He says if you're making this fuel formula available to everyone then there's nothing stopping someone trying to artificially manipulate the markets so they ultimately corner the value - whatever you want or try and do. And if the Governor wants to help someone do that, especially if he solves a great chunk of his own problems, he can make life pretty well unbearable."

"Do you think I should come out and see him?" asked Brian, his heavy schedule of commitments very much in his mind but this was as serious as things could get.

"I don't know that you can do anything. But if you don't try we'll never know. So the answer has to be yes."

Brian sighed. "OK. I'll let you know as soon as I can how quickly I can be with you."

Chapter 6

It was not that long ago that to enter the Houses of Parliament in London involved the relatively simply process of approaching via St Stephen's Gate, nodding politely at the gentlemen of the law and especially the one with the light machine gun, showing one's authority or invitation, passing through the simplest of security scans, up the stairs, into the building and more or less walking straight into Central Lobby. But with terrorism raising its ugly head - and seemingly especially since the only-just-failed attempt to drive a large 4WD vehicle loaded with explosive fuels into the front of Glasgow airport, it was no longer quite that simple.

Bond was pondering this as he settled behind a small queue of people waiting to enter via the new route. It was then his mobile phone went off. It could hardly have been a more inconvenient moment. It was early morning. He was very weary and feeling particularly belligerent. It was raining. It was cold. And he could not find the wretched phone in his pockets. One or two people ahead of him turned to see who was causing the disturbance.

Bond had driven down from the Scottish North coast to Inverness and caught a flight to London the night before. He had had a bad night in an over-hot but cheap hotel bedroom, got up early, skipped breakfast and was now standing in the small queue on the gentle slope that leads down to the more extensive security everyone is now obliged to pass through. Once visitors have nodded at the policemen at St. Stephen's Gate, they now take a sharp left turn and walk downhill towards a more testing system that often includes a full bod search. On busy days the queue of people waiting to be checked can reach back to the outside pavement where visitors have to stand unprotected from the elements.

But today only a few early visitors were seeking entrance. Bond was pleased to reach the covered walkway that now leads to the security check. It had been cold and damp walking across Parliament Square past the QE Conference Centre, the open space having a mist-like appearance this morning. A persistent and penetrating fine rain drifted across the square like ground level clouds, soaking everyone but especially the one or two protestors and their flags and banners located on the grass opposite the seat of Government. It was the sort of miserable morning that sees imposing and historic buildings that can shine and glitter in great magnificence on sunny days turn drab and grey on mornings like this. Rush hour commuters look even drabber, greyer and more miserable than usual, and the city pigeons look wet, dejected and dishevelled as they peck around the puddles for scraps of food.

Bond swore under his breath and fumbled amongst his pockets to find the phone, trying to do so before it switched to voicemail. He stood aside to let other shufflers in the queue go by as he discovered who was phoning at this most inconvenient of moments.

"Detective Inspector McLeod, Mr Bond." The voiced was deep and guttural - and very Scottish. "I hope I've not caught you at an inconvenient moment. Perhaps a little early, Mr Bond?"

Bond grunted a response. It was, he agreed, far too early.

"I'm afraid I have some bad news for you Sir," said the policeman who only 24 hours ago had had to be persuaded by Bond to let him leave Northern Scotland to attend an important meeting with the Climate Change Committee Chairman and others in the House of Commons. The Inspector had been impressed with the reason for the journey but still stressed that Bond was significantly part of a triple murder enquiry. There had been a lively discussion which was not so much an argument but more a robust dialogue. The Detective Inspector had eventually succumbed to Bond's request on agreement that Bond keep close telephone contact with the DI.

On this grey and dull morning the DI's gruff and deep voice seemed to match the gloom.

"I'm afraid, Mr Bond, your cottage in Caithness has been turned over. Someone - though we suspect there was more than one - has been through it from one end to the other with a fine tooth comb. Obviously searching for something. Or maybe someone. It's not difficult to guess they were searching for you. Whatever they were trying to find, they left one hell of a mess. I'm sorry."

Bond's heart sank. But the news got worse.

"The trouble is, Mr Bond," the gruff Scottish voice continued. "I'm thinking - if the people who did this are the same people involved who perpetrated the inn massacre, they're a very dangerous lot. And the obvious truth is that it is likely to be the same lot. And I worry what might have become of you had you been there."

The same thought had already crossed Bond's mind.

"And," continued the detective, "I wonder what they were looking for? If they haven't found it in your cottage, clearly it places you in a very difficult position. And now, Mr Bond, I worry that they may know about your place in the Midlands. Or might they even know where you are now? And what about your family?"

All of that had not crossed Bond's mind.

"And although I can express worry for your wellbeing, I'm not sure what I can do to protect you when we are, at this stage, guessing and with no real idea of these people's motives or who they are. And, you are a very mobile person, Mr Bond, as we discussed yesterday."

The policeman paused for breath.

"The only thing I can do, Mr Bond, is caution you to be on your guard and vigilant. Be very vigilant. I have your address in the Midlands and officers are on their way as we speak to check that it's still secure. As soon as I can, I'll let you know. Meantime, Mr Bond, take care. Take great care."

Bond felt the cold, wet miserable morning take on another bleak dimension. He shivered involuntarily and re-joined the queue. There was still not that many people in it because of the early hour and the visitors shuffled steadily towards the awaiting security check. Once X-rayed and searched, Bond was exposed to the miserable elements once more for the short walk in the open leading to the grand entrance to Westminster Hall.

Bond went through the security process without really realising it. His mind was in a whirl and he felt slightly sick.

Once out of the rain and into the enormity of Westminster Hall, he checked his watch which confirmed he was significantly early for his meeting. It gave him the opportunity to walk to the towering left wall and to one of the few benches, unoccupied at this early hour. Later, this magnificent space, the oldest building in Parliament and almost the only part of the ancient Palace of Westminster to survive, would be full of tourists and little groups of people having ad hoc meetings. Bond, a not infrequent visitor to Parliament, had always thought this entrance was by far a more appropriate and superior one than had previously been used. Westminster Hall, once the largest hall in Europe, was steeped in antiquity and often conjured in his mind historic images such as that when the deceased Queen Mother had lain in waiting for her public to pay its last respects. More than 1000 years of parliamentary democracy was embroiled within the echoing chasms and arches of this most English of places.

Bond flopped onto one of the benches, bent forward, his head in his hands. It was a good place for him to sit and contemplate events. He felt empty - worried sick - not a little frightened - enormously frustrated that events were beyond his control. How had this mess happened? What had it got to do with him? Who were these people? How could he stop them? What did they want?

In his 50 years Bond had never encountered any experience that had parallel or close resemblance to this current plight. Flashbacks to the scene in the inn were frequent and he had thought a thousand times about the people he had seen meeting at the inn - the day all the papers flew about. That seemed to be the nub of it. He had meticulously gone through his own papers afterwards and found he had inadvertently picked up a blank letterhead of a company called Asian Pacific Trading Inc. There was nothing written on the letterhead but there was a QR code which, when Bond tried to scan it and activate it, proved to be unlockable. It did nothing. He had handed the blank document in to the police but had kept a note of the company name and the address in China.

He worried about what had happened to his cottage in Scotland. He worried about what might happen to his house in the Midlands. Fortunately his bachelor status meant there was no close family to be concerned about.

Thoughts ran through his mind at a million miles an hour but offered him no solutions, only the problem. He felt helpless and in a cul-de-sac of despair. He sat, head still in his hands, in the echoing, dank, cathedral-like enormity of Westminster Hall.

"Bond."

"Bond." The second call of his name shook him from his deep thinking and he looked up. Ted Butler was just a few feet away. Conservative Member of Parliament but, more significantly to Bond, Chairman of the All Party Climate Change Committee. He and Butler had known each other for years.

"Bloody hell Bond, I thought you were asleep. And God knows - you look awful. You ok?"

The question was obviously rhetorical because the MP did not wait for a reply before he continued, "But if you're going to come and talk to us you'd better wake up and get yourself into action. You look ghastly. But we must move if you want to talk to us. The three of us haven't got much time".

Wearily, Bond stood from the bench and together they walked to the end of the hall and up the room-wide ancient stone steps to the top where they turned left and passed through Central Lobby with the House of Commons to the left and the House of Lords to the right. At the end of the walkway a sleepy looking policeman nodded to them before they walked down the stairs to the room adjacent Dining Room 1. The meeting had been arranged there because the three MPs Bond was about to talk to were involved in a morning meeting in the Dining Room. The room into which they now entered was wood panelled except for the full length window with glass doors that open on to the balcony the other side of which is the River Thames.

Dick Fellows, Labour MP and Ali Rashed, Liberal MP, together with Ted Butler headed up this All Party Committee. Bond knew them well and he was highly respected by them. Persistent and very anguished pleas from Bond had eventually achieved this meeting. Now, with the opportunity before him, but with his passion drained and gone, he felt deflated and with no zeal or energy or zest for talking to these people. There was no enthusiasm left for this at all. All he wanted to do was crawl away and hide somewhere.

But here he was and they expected him to deliver. This was a rare opportunity and he would have to do his best. He had fought to get this meeting, driven by anguish, anger, frustration, despair and a growing sense of futility.

Bond had what to him was a desperate message for the three Members of Parliament. New evidence from the scientific community still showed growing pollution into the globe's atmosphere, despite a world-wide recession. It had been thought the recession would mean less manufacturing, less vehicles on the road, less aircraft movements - therefore less polluting activity. But the world-wide economic downturn - except in China, India, Brazil and a few other countries, had seen global pollution continuing to rise. Levels were still increasing. Scientific expeditions to the Arctic and Greenland showed the ice caps melting faster than ever before and at an alarmingly increasing rate.

But that was not the only problem. The world's population continued to grow - at a rate never experienced before. And while millions of people remained without proper food, heating and shelter, ironically and in parallel to the misery of these millions, others in equal number were becoming new members of the consumer society, massively increasing the pressure on global resources. The chase for what resources there are on the planet continued to accelerate with some countries getting desperate and some, notably China, buying up stocks around the world. Both the demand for energy and the amounts of discarded waste continued to climb.

Bond took a deep breath and started.

"I don't know whether this is futile or not. I am truly fed up with talking and not seeing any action. But you three have significant influence and anyway you're the most influential politicians I know. But in the last 20 years, despite all the rhetoric, the good and well intended words, committee after committee after committee, two Rio Global Summits, the Kyoto Protocol, the COP process - and ten and tens of thousands of people attending these events at enormous financial cost and God knows what in terms of carbon emissions, and all the pledges and even new laws - despite all this - by every measure we know our species on this planet is heading in the wrong direction and in many instances we are at - or close to - crisis point - the well discussed tipping point - a moment when we go past the point when retrieval no longer remains a prospect and we slide uncontrollably towards oblivion ."

"Yet our politics is dominated by the Treasury and short termism. I can't believe we've had elections in the UK, in America and in other advanced nations where hardly a word has been spoken about what some of us think is the most important issue we're facing - potentially the most critical point in the history of mankind. Our governments tag on responses to these challenges almost as an afterthought."

He looked closely at the MPs, trying to gauge if this was having any reaction on them at all. They seemed to be heeding what he was saying but he wondered if they really were. They had heard all this before from him - from others - and many times. Was this yet another moment of forlorn hope? He continued:

"What we need is a government that takes an integrated view and undertakes a fundamental response to the most important set of challenges ever to hit our species on this planet. And Parliament knows that. We've had reports from people like former Chief Scientist John Beddington and world leading economist Nick Stern. They've created little impact. Certainly there's not been an action based response to the scale and magnitude they called for."

"And we have reacted to those reports," Ted Butler interrupted, "Give credit where credit is due, Bond. A lot's happening."

"Oh, come on Ted," Bond replied, "You know as well as I do that we're not doing enough. We're just playing at the edges. You know - how come you guys here in the seat of Government can decide - almost overnight - to spend - what was it - three million million pounds to save the banks? An unprecedented action in peace time. You grabbed money. You printed money. You wrote cheques overnight. The speed of response and the colossal size of the expenditure was breathtaking. Truly amazing! All to save the banks after the so-called credit crunch. Yet you can't find the money Nick Stern told you to spend to combat climate change. It's unbelievable!"

"The World Bank reckons it cost 13% of GDP to save the banks. You spent that. Nick Stern estimated it would cost 1% of GDP to potentially save our species on this planet. But you couldn't spend that. Where the hell is the intelligence in that? Where's the right priority? What's the matter with you people?"

Ali Rashed tried to say something but Bond was flying now, getting angrier as he developed his case. He cut the Liberal MP short.

"And where's saving the banks got us? Across Europe and elsewhere we've got failing currencies and failing economies. Cut backs in expenditure to try and pull nations out of unbelievable amounts of debt are creating social havoc. So where did government social responsibility go I wonder? How do you answer the youth of today who have no jobs, no money, no future and no hope? I'm amazed the streets of Europe aren't on fire with disenfranchised and disillusioned youngsters rebelling against the inadequacies of a pathetic political structure and sterile politicians. How do you answer the old folk whose savings, if they've had any, are been whittled away by the declining value of currencies?"

"As I've said before, there's so much to be gained from an integrated response - a Green Economy response where finding and implementing solutions to these massive, species-threatening challenges can create new businesses – stimulate innovation - create new jobs - generate taxes that then enables you as a Parliament to do the things a socially responsible government should do - like looking after the sick and the elderly and ensuring our children are properly educated. A green economy supported by well placed investment and appropriate legislation".

"The Liberal Party has always championed such things," said Ali Rashed. "And we work hard to ensure Government actions represent these issues."

"Oh, bollocks!" responded Bond with the anger in his voice growing. "Come on Ali. You must be joking! If you lot were as good as you say you are, why are all the indicators going in the wrong direction? For God's sake, wake up! Stop fooling yourselves! For once, look outside the political bubble and see the real world. What is needed is a radical new approach, not piecemeal, timid responses. But timid, half baked, badly thought out, knee jerk responses are what you lot keep delivering."

"Now come on Gene. That's pretty strong and ingenuous," challenged Butler.

"No it bloody isn't," barked back Bond. "It's the truth. And it may hurt. You lot might not like it. But what we desperately need, before it's too late, is positive, top-priority response and leadership on a global scale. The UK can't resolve these issues on its own but it could use its influence to encourage a global response. It can't do that and behave the way it currently is. That would be the epitome of hypocrisy. Not that I'm sure politics can resolve these challenges. Politics is mostly based on local thinking and short termism. What we need is a co-ordinated global response and long-term planning. The UN is proving to be close on useless."

"I think you're overstating the negatives," said Butler. "And anyway, what would you have us do that we're not already doing?"

Bond shrugged his shoulders. "God knows. We are in such a mess I can only implore you people to stop thinking of this as a peripheral issue to what you consider to be the important things of life - which is almost exclusively about money and growth. There can be nothing more important than this! My plea to you three who head an influential part of government is to support the case for a radical new, green economic approach. We've had opportunities to transform the way we run and manage our country. It could have been a global exemplar. But it's nothing like that. All you offer is sticking plaster solutions - sticking your finger in the leaking dyke! It's not strategic. It's not mainstream. It's not only sad. It's a monstrous fucking disaster."

He glared at them - challenging for a response.

Ali Rashed spoke.

"You're always inspiring, Gene. Always challenging. As often as not you're right. And it's timely to say these things to us. I know Dick and Ted and I will all want to represent what you say at the next All Party Committee."

Bond looked at them in silence for a while, then lowered and shook his head. When he spoke it was almost in a whisper and in a tone of resigned failure.

"Committee. Committee. Is that all you people can think about? I'm here this morning because time is running out. We're facing a calamitous disaster and all you people can do is talk about it. I keep telling you the same things - you sympathise - but nothing happens. Quite frankly I've come to the conclusion that politics is only about short termism, your own survival - and votes. It's a load of bollocks and I'm wasting my time."

And, to the surprise of the three Members of Parliament, and with no further word to them, he stood and walked away, head down, shoulders drooped. The politicians stared after him in disbelief.

Chapter 7

In a dingy, dark, partly cobblestoned East London street lined by tall, lifeless and seemingly derelict buildings with broken windows and crumbling brickwork, red and blue neon lights break the darkness to proclaim to the outside world that here is the Russian Bar. They shine 24 hours a day, evidence that this establishment of dubious reputation provides a round the clock refuge for anyone looking for escapism in the unique form it serves.

To gain entry you either have to be a member, be a guest of a member, or have enough cash to bribe your way in. Access is via a door so heavy it would do justice as a side entrance to a castle. As a fortification it looks as if there should be a facility above it from which to pour hot pitch and tar. Fortunately there is not but in every other respect it looks medieval and capable of being well defended . Seemingly of solid oak reinforced by ancient metal strips, the door has an eye level reinforced grill that opens from the inside to enable someone that side of the door to see who is on the other.

On the pavement side, and to the right of the door, is a brass knob which, when pulled, sounds a bell inside. Visitors have to have faith that something, sometime is going to happen because there is no audible confirmation outside that the bell has rung inside. A response to the pull of the knob often seems to take eternity and many a disillusioned visitor has turned away thinking nothing was going to happen. Patience is always rewarded - eventually - when the sound of bolts being slid heralds the arrival of someone. With a clatter, the grill opens and a set of eyes can be seen. A voice grunts some uninterruptable words and if the response is right, or the amount of cash offered is big enough, the grill shuts with a slam and the full door opens.

Once access has been achieved a newcomer faces a set of worn and grubby carpeted steps leading upwards to the bar. Bond had gained entrance by telling the set of eyes at the open grill of the door that he was there as a guest of Georgi Patarava.

As Bond entered the noise was almost deafening and the atmosphere thick with smoke. The Russian Bar has never caught up with modern laws of no smoking inside buildings. The smell of Belomorkanals, together with other smoked substances of even lesser legality, permeated the air to create a thick, swirling thickness. The bar and those within it were being beaten almost into submission by the alarmingly deafening noise of deep South American rock and roll. Dictating the choice of music was a man standing behind the bar whose frizzy hair dominated his whole physique, almost obliterating his body shape as it cascaded off his head in huge, white dyed volume.

Opposite the bar the area divides into two - a small dance area and an equally small eating area. As Bond surveyed the scene the latter was currently empty. The dance floor was occupied by two young girls, both tall and shapely and with little clothing, vigorously moving their youthful bodies to the music in alcohol encouraged abandonment.

Bond saw Georgi sitting at the bar at the same time as Georgi saw him. Georgi rose to welcome his guest with a breath sapping bear hug. The man behind the bar nodded in recognition.

This was by no means Bond's first visit here. Georgi and he had spent many hours talking about what seemed like profound global issues whilst getting hugely drunk. That is why Bond was here now. This was the last place on the planet to be under normal circumstances but the first place to be to gain solace from reality and to depart company, at least for a while, with the real world and its problems. In fact, the first time Georgi had suggested they meet at the Russian Bar Bond had raised his eyebrows in some surprise.

"You - in a Russian Bar?" he had asked in some astonishment. Georgi normally hated anything associated with Russia.

"It's only a name," his Georgian friend had responded. "It's owned by Arabs and run by an old friend of mine. But it serves the best vodka in town."

Bond had first met Georgi when they were much younger when Georgi was an Assistant Commercial Attache for the Soviet Embassy in London. They had met several times at the Attache's offices based in the Georgian elegance of a palatial house in Knightsbridge. Bond always remembered his first visit there, being led by a secretary to a front room with its grand fireplace over which hung an enormous watercolour painting. He mistook it to be a picture of a circa 1950s Bedford coach heading down a main road with the sea and beaches to the left. There was a tower in the distance that looked distinctly like the Blackpool Tower. The whole scene had an 'English seaside' feel to it with the main focal point being a typical coach of the time which, in their day - Bond recalled - were known as charabancs. It instantly brought back nostalgic memories of being a toddler on holiday with his parents. The giveaway on the painting was that the traffic was on the wrong side of the road. It was that that caused him to enquire about the scene. He found the painting was nothing to do with an English view but depicted a scene on a main road heading out of Moscow.

"Strange," he had thought to himself at the time "how we think we are all so different - how we build such divides between us - yet so often we find we have so many similarities."

Initial contact with Georgi was on a business footing. Bond was researching environmental issues in the aftermath of the Cold War - a period known to some as the 'tanks to ploughs' period. As relationships between East and West that had been cold for years started to thaw, environmentalists hoped military manufacturing resources and the materials they used would be turned from making war machines to making machines to increase food production for an ever increasingly hungry world.

The two men had struck an immediate friendship. Their meetings always strayed far and wide across political, environmental and social issues and would be to the accompaniment of the unfettered consumption of Georgian brandy - Caucasus brandy to be specific. When, at their first, meeting Bond had commented on the taste and smoothness of the drink, Georgi Patarava had picked up the bottle and read from the label in a colourful, theatrical style accompanied by stage-like flamboyant waves of his free arm and hand.

"It attracts by its history, its grandeur, hospitality, beauty of women and nature, braveness of men, love to feasts, respect of guests, polyphony songs and hot dances."

"That's my kind of drink!" Bond had agreed and quite quickly the two men had become friends, realising that they had many interests in common - politics, the environment, women and drink. Their friendship had lasted several years, a period of great worldly events such as the unification of West and East Berlin following the breath taking speed by which the Berlin wall had fallen. It gave them much to talk about.

There had been a time when Bond had thought he had lost Georgi as a friend, drinking companion and confidant.

"We may not meet again after today," Georgi had told Bond. "We are heading towards very dark and troubled times. I may not survive. When it happens, remember Bond, I am a Georgian."

Bond had asked what he meant but his friend had changed the subject. Not long afterwards the Soviet Union had collapsed and the Embassy in London became that of Russia. Georgi disappeared from Bond's life and the memory of their friendship faded until, a little later, his reference to "dark and troubled times" came to Bond's mind as he read that Russia was at war with Georgia. Was that what Georgi had meant by his cryptic remark? That five day war brought back strong and warm memories of Georgi who he assumed had died in the bloody and uncompromising conflict with the Russians. He was amazed and delighted when - as if fate had pulled them together again - some years later he had found he was sitting next to Georgi at a conference in Frankfurt.

"What happened to you? I thought you were dead?" asked Bond.

"I thought I was dead too," replied the Georgean. "In fact I think I died many times during that bloody time. I sometimes think I am dead now."

Despite Bond's digging, Georgi would say little about the conflict with the Russians. But he did find that Georgi was now freelancing as a link between Eastern European nations, newly freed from their former Soviet masters, and the EU which they aspired to join. The friendship took off again as if there had never been any interrupting gap years, and Georgi became a haven in Bond's life - someone to turn to when there was a need to unload the problems of the world when they seemed to be overwhelming - as they often had done and as they certainly did now. They did not meet often but when they did the kindred spirit between them was always healthy. From very different beginnings and backgrounds, they had so much in common, so many similar frustrations about worldly matters, distrust and impatience with bureaucratic machinery and politicians especially.

The staple drink at the Russian bar is ice-cold - near freezing - Russian vodka chasers, served in long stemmed silver goblets with white frozen sugar rims and slammed down between gulps of dark beer.

Georgi realised very quickly that his friend was in a bad state and it took only a few goblets and some beer before the story started to unfold. Because it was fresh in his mind, Bond recounted with some venom the frustrations of his meeting with the MPs.

"Ah, yes - politicians," Georgi nearly spat the word out. "Not to be trusted. The scourge of mankind!"

It would have been easy for the two of them to let the get together degenerate into a politician bashing episode, fuelled by vodka and beer. But the real story Bond wanted to unleash to his friend was the happenings in the remote inn in

Scotland. It was only when Bond mentioned Asian Pacific Trading Inc that Georgi interrupted.

"APTI?"

"Yes, do you know them?"

"I know of them" said Georgi. "They have Russian connections."

"I thought they're Chinese. They're a Chinese procurement agency," Bond responded.

"You may be right. But they certainly have Russian connections. Tell me the rest of your story and we'll come back to that."

Bond did as requested - right up to the telephone call from the police when he was standing in the line of people outside the Palace of Westminster. And when he had finished he said "OK - tell me more about what you know about APTI."

Which Georgi did. There was not much to tell. Georgi had been involved in a technology intellectual property issue between a UK university and one in China when he first encountered APTI.

"They were quite helpful and very knowledgeable," he recalled. "But because it looked as if they might get involved with the business transactions I was working on, I did a history search on them. And though on the surface they looked fine - enough to satisfy most people doing standard business searches - I decided to dig a bit more. Or at least I tried to but I hit some serious and sophisticated barriers. Not the sort of barriers that are there by accident. These were top jobs - very professional - state-of-the-art. The sort the military might use. I didn't like that and it worried me."

"So I delved some more and I found APTI is linked somehow to another company that I know - SDBI, which is South Korea based and also has some murky corners to it. Sustainable Development Broking International does a lot of good and legitimate work. But there is something decidedly dodgy about it somewhere. But I hadn't got much time then and they were only involved on the fringes of the transaction so I didn't bother to investigate them further though I promised myself to do so sometime. I sort of logged it as incomplete business and something to do when I had more time."

"Do you feel like digging around a bit now?" asked Bond.

"Maybe," said his Georgian friend. "And while all this craziness is in your life, why don't you come and stay with me? It may not be luxurious but it'll be safe and I have a fine range of Vodka."

It took Bond only seconds to accept the invitation and with that they settled down to the task of getting inebriated whilst watching the dancing girls, one of whom was now topless and whose breasts, glistening with sweat, flayed around as the young girl flaunted her body to the beat of the music.

It was in the early hours of the morning when they left, the heavy door of the club crashing behind them as they walked out into a dying night with the first shades of morning beginning to appear. It was drizzling again and Bond hoped the taxi they had ordered would not be long coming. He was relieved to first hear - then see - a car round the nearby bend and come into sight, headlights blazing and the rain drenched road glistening as it approached.

He and Georgi took a step forward towards the car but then he felt Georgi's arm tighten on his own and a pull of immense strength which caused him to topple and crash into the body of Georgi which was heading in the same direction - downwards. As his body hit both pavement and Georgi simultaneously he heard a series of rapid explosions then the unmistakable, ear splitting sound of a gun being fired right next to him. Georgi - he immediately realised - was shooting at the taxi!

Chapter 8

It was a cold, windy but sparklingly clear and beautiful day and some months before the fateful shooting in a remote Scottish inn. The taxi drive from the university took him to the suspension bridge over which he walked to Tatyshev Island. The Yenisei river looked superb and provided a moving and ever changing strip of rich blue with crystal white tops where the wind rippled its surface. Once on the island, the pathway was bordered with beds of plants that would be a sea of rosehips by the summer. Across the river, the city of Krasnoyarsk glistened in its full glory as if to substantiate a claim made by many that it truly is the most beautiful city in Siberia.

There were not many people in the park this time of the morning. It was cold, around minus 10 degrees he guessed, and the breeze gave an edge to the coldness. He pulled his trench coat tighter around him and pulled the collar up. It was still early in the day and most who were out and about were enthusiastic youngsters exercising their growing bodies. By far the majority were students. Some were probably from his own faculty though he would not recognise many so vast was the array of educational institutes that made Krasnoyarsk a globally recognised centre of advanced education.

Viktor Blucher made his way to the tea room. Now 70 years of age, he tended to feel the cold more these days though the walks in the morning did his body and soul good, as long as the weather remained dry. His arthritic joints did not like the wet or the damp. He was pleased that this year's annual reunion was in his home city. Travel was less attractive now and sometimes quite painful and wearying and certainly less exciting than it used to be. Let the others come to him for a change.

Only four of them were left now to meet every year on the same day - November 9th - as they had done since that prophetic day in 1989. That day they considered to be one of madness that saw the wall torn down by the people of both East and West Berlin and which opened the sluice gate to let the unbelievable happened - the collapse of the Soviet Union. Like a wildfire through a dry forest, the zest for freedom had spread at an incredible pace across Eastern Europe, breaking political bonds that had been tied for decades and releasing people to reshape their own destinies. Now the four of them would meet in perpetuation of the annual tribute to the past and to pay homage to those who were no longer with them.

Born into a peasant family in central Russia, Viktor had joined the army to escape poverty. He had become an artillery officer in the Red Army, had shown great military tactical understanding and risen rapidly through the ranks. His skills and his outspoken devotion to the Union made him sufficiently visible to be plucked out of the army's clutches and into the world of the Chekists, subterfuge and espionage specialists so named after the 1920s Cheka terror organisation.

His military career took him to the rank of Supreme Officer and he operated in the dirty shadows of the cold war in many parts of the world and in many different organisations including the KGB and then the FSB before he retired, eventually finding part-time work lecturing on global politics in what was originally the Siberian Federal University. This academic base was highly convenient. It provided part time work in Krasnoyarsk to which he had moved many years ago and which he now considered to be his home. It provided an income to supplement his army pension. And it was especially useful now because of Krasnoyarsk's large Chinese immigrant population and large numbers of Chinese students at the university. That provided a highly effective disguise for Viktor's less public, less palatable activities, especially those linked to China.

But the bitterness of the massive betrayals and subsequent rapid collapse of the Soviet Union remained within him like a cancer. As it did with his fellow ex-Chekists of which only three others now survived from the original group of 10.

Now their annual meeting saw them reflect on a world that had been overtaken by new events, to wallow in nostalgic memories from days when they were in their prime, in control - in command.

There was no leader to the group and in its infancy there had been no agenda save for meeting once a year to rekindle the bonding of close comrades. But the common despair, fuelled annually by their reminiscing back to days of former glory, slowly gave gestation to an idea that was at first a seed and an inkling but which grew to become an ambition then an obsession. Its basic goal was revenge.

This regular annual event was of no particular value to anyone but the group involved. It based its existence primarily on nostalgia. But that took a turn to become something extremely different when the group's new found obsession met money. Viktor had taken one of the sponsors of the course he delivered at the University to the tea shop on the island in the middle of the river that flowed through the city. There had been no particular motive behind the move. No expectation it would lead to anything. It had been a gesture of courtesy and thanks to a sponsor.

He just happened, in general conversation, to tell his guest how he and his three friends, survivors of the original band of ten, met annually. He told him how, when they came to Tatyshev Island - this small island paradise in the middle of this Siberian river, they would drink tea from a copper samovar. And in the tranquil, relatively quiet but bitterly cold environment of Tatyshev Island they, as they always did wherever they met, would reminisce over glorious days gone by and re-examine and scrutinise the reasons why their world had collapsed. Could Yeltsin have done things differently? Could he have remodelled the Soviet Union? Could the blight of widespread corruption have been broken? Could the catastrophic economic disaster, an aftermath of World War 2 compounded afterwards by the massive costs involved in the so called arms race with the West and the space race with America, have been successfully dealt with? There were schools of thought that said he could have won these battles, over time. But, in 1991, Yeltsin had, under particular pressure from the governments of the Ukraine and Belarus, signed the Belavezha Accords which disbanded the Soviet Union.

Yeltsin had been aware that the Union was cracking - that break up was virtually inevitable. It was, to him, only a question of when. Then, like a finger being withdrawn from a hole in a dyke, on the night of November 9th 1989 an East German official had inadvertently announced that crossings to the West would be opening. Thousands of East Berliners lined up at checkpoints in the Berlin Wall. They, together with mass crowds on the West side of the wall, took freedom into their own hands and tore down the global symbol of the great divide between the free Western world and the struggling Communist states of the Union. With guards powerless and without orders, the wall gave way and East and West Berlin united in a gushing of patriotic emotion that was witnessed across the world.

In Moscow these events were viewed in horror but there was little or nothing they could do and Yeltsin and his government could only see the action in Berlin fuel discontent that had been growing from Moscow to the far Eastern reaches of the once mighty empire.

To the old guard such as Viktor Blucher, the demise was hardly unexpected but still utterly unpalatable. Factions of the military tried to rebel against the political tide of events but the sweep of rebellion was too great. The collapse came and people like Viktor and his comrades were stuck in it as if in a time warp.

Viktor and his guest had talked chess to begin with. It was safe common territory for small talk. It broke the ice between two men who hardly knew each other. It transpired they both shared a passion for the game. As the relationship warmed it encouraged Viktor to be more adventurous with what he was saying. And slowly he got round to telling the old guards' story to his guest with some caution, explained their ambitions, fruitless though they might be because they could never be fulfilled. He only provided an outline. One never knew how others would respond, where their sympathies might lie. It was, he said in almost apology, a fruitless exercise, this reminiscing, this annual return to the past, this futile examination of what might have been. But Viktor and his three remaining friends took some solace from it and at least delighted in recalling names of old comrades long since departed.

To his surprise, his guest, Boris Koslov, showed much interest. He himself was a former military man. He had moved into the oil industry. Fate had dealt him a good hand and that, plus some agile thinking and fast and opportunist actions, saw the ex-military man become one of Russia's new family of Oligarchs. It was because of this Viktor had a basic dislike of Boris. Boris was the epitome of the new Russia that had become disgustingly and mega wealthy very quickly and at massive cost to others. Viktor, and the surviving group of aged military men, despised this new breed of rich Muscovites. But that did not stop them using their money, as Viktor did with funds from Boris to support his university course.

Boris had listened intently and with much sympathy to what Viktor had told him but had not said much in response. Viktor was left wondering if he had bored Boris with his story or if indeed Boris had totally different thoughts to theirs. So it came as a considerable surprise when, some weeks later, Boris made another visit to the University. This was unusual. He normally only visited once a year. And he insisted they again visit the island. There Boris outlined an idea to Viktor which Viktor eventually took to his surviving friends. Together they took their venomous recollections of the past, their hatred of the demise of the old regime, and hatched what they called with deference to the game of chess - 'The Final Check Mate' or 'Shah Mat' in Russian. The final Shah Mat would be an appropriate final act by this stalwart group that represented standards of a long departed era. Now, while they despised the fact that arguably the new Russia wielded more global power and influence than had ever been achieved by the old Soviet Union, the combination of their own final dreams and this Oligarch's money was too attractive an idea and would realise ambitions the four of them had had for years but had had little hope of delivering. They had the contacts and influences to make it happen. Boris had the money. They would use chess as a basis for coded communications. And though they could not dismiss from their mutual consciousness that it was highly hypocritical to use corrupted oil money to lubricate the wheels of their own plot, they could not resist the temptation. Together with Boris they committed to deliver the final Shah Mat.

Viktor had used his University connections to develop useful contacts both in China and South Korea as the scheme developed. Their new-found oil tycoon provided a constant flow of money to loosen a few strategically useful and corruptible officials right across the eastern world. And now as they sat supping their tea and reviewing 'The Final Shah Mat' project which had started nearly a year ago, they formed the general consensus that they were on target and on time. It was, they felt, time to just watch developments.

Chapter 9

UC Irvine - the University of California, founded in 1965 and located in the Orange County of Southern California, like many other academic institutions around the world, works hard and diligently to ensure that across its 21 acres of research projects and countless ambitious academics and students, there is maintained an effective cross fertilisation of ideas between its wide ranging faculties. Like all such institutes, success in this ambition is mixed. Located in the tree scattered areas of the Daniel Aldrich Park, its centres of academic and research excellence are housed in smart, if somewhat clinical and sterile modern, white concrete buildings. And like all academic institutions UC Irvine struggles to ensure the faculties don't function in glorious isolation but actively seek to co-operate with each other. It's not easy. But it's not easy in the complex structures of any major centre of research and academic activity.

What many thought to be a 'eureka moment' happened comparatively recently when the work of the University's Advanced Power and Energy Programme, funded in part by the California Energy Commission's Alternative and Renewable Fuel and Vehicle Technology programme, and the aged but energetic and passionate Brian Kemp in England, linked to the work on nanotechnology of the Henry Samueli School of Engineering, also part of the University.

Part of that nanotechnology research by the university was aimed at increasing the effectiveness of catalysts to enhance the conversion of raw materials into fuel. It was found to have major production benefits in the processes Brian Kemp was playing with in the separation of hydrogen and oxygen in CO_2. The result was a co-ordinated partnership approach to accelerate the development of the Kemp idea, one which was taking the laboratory production into the world of commercial volume manufacturing - just what Kemp had been striving to achieve.

Some observers said the outcome of the link between the two University initiatives and Kemp's programme in England was, perhaps, the 'quantum leap' the world was waiting for. Rumours were rife. The media was becoming increasingly interested though all involved were trying to maintain a wall of silence until they were sure their endeavours had worked.

Now, on this sunny day, the meeting was being held in the Chancellor's office. It had all been organised in a rush and at the demand of the White House. The President was insistent that he wanted immediate discussions about the Chinese offer to California even though the Governor was equally keen to keep the whole matter away from central administration. Al Williams was highly protective of his own position but eventually had bowed to pressure when the President himself intervened on a person to person call and demanded a face to face discussion. Williams was equally adamant that those with vested interests should be present.

So assembled in what could be sensed right from the start to be a very tense get together were President Jack Thompson accompanied by industrialist Max Trueman from his inner sanctum, the Englishman Brian Kemp, Governor Williams, and Chancellor Susan Williamson. The President had demanded that all secretaries and aids be dismissed and that no notes be taken.

"The reason we're meeting is for me - as President - to personally understand what is going on here. I want to investigate this myself. I want to get a first-hand appreciation of what's going on here. That should tell you how important this is to me. It is your President that stands before you. Not his officials or aids."

"Let me be clear from the outset that I'm angry and don't take kindly to being kept in the dark about a potential deal that is of national significance. I don't care for it when a matter of potential national importance comes to my attention courtesy of the Washington Post!"

He almost spat the name of the newspaper then waited momentarily to let the point drive home. He continued: "I believe the proposed deal we are here to talk about involves outputs from this university and also from Mr Kemp's organisation in England. That is why we are here in your office Madam Chancellor and why I invited Mr Kemp to be here. I'm grateful Mr Kemp for your efforts in travelling here at short notice."

Brian Kemp nodded in acknowledgement to the President, who continued.

"As I understand it, there is negotiation in hand between the State of California and the Government of China for China to provide oil to California in return for access to technology originating from this University."

"My first objective is to find out if my understanding is right. If it is, I - no, we - have a problem because such a deal would be diametrically opposed to my new national policy on energy charging if such a deal makes California think it can opt out. Let me make it crystal clear. The new scheme we have proposed is crucial to the nation at a time of national economic plight. The nation is in a critical - perilous - economic state. The move as proposed here, if what I hear is right, could be a serious threat to our recovery plans. The flow of cheap oil into California might seem like an idea to be welcomed. But it has massive downsides. It would throw markets into chaos, would skew values, be grossly unfair to other States in the Union, and it would deny tax to the Federal Government which is essential if we are to continue to function as a socially conscious, cohesive and effective national government. It could set precedents that could rock way beyond the whole boat. In my mind, it could take us to the brink of a precipice which could be of unfathomable disasters."

"It also raises the question - what is the motive of China? It also has its energy supply problems, greater than our own. Its fast growth economy is screaming for more energy. So why would they give anything away? And if they - the Chinese - think what they're getting back is of greater value, then I'd hope we too would consider that value and check before we do anything to ensure we're not handing out something we will regret later. The baby and bathwater come to mind."

"So I am asking you is my interpretation of the facts right?"

Williams and Chancellor Williamson both tried to respond at the same time but it was the politician who won the stage.

"My challenge, Mr President, is that at a time when my State is virtually bankrupt, someone has come along with a solution I cannot ignore. I have to balance local Californian interests against those of the Nation. The approach was made to me direct, as Governor of the State of California. It was an unsolicited approach. It came out of the blue. We were certainly not looking for it. How could we have? It was not addressed to the President and it was not a deal offered on a national basis. It was - er, it is - a parochial, Californian issue. So my problem is, Mr President, what do I say to my people if they know I've got access to cheap sources of energy? Do I say - "Sorry guys. I can't do the deal with the Chinese because the President says so. And by the way, the President also wants you to pay more for your gas anyway!"

"But as I understand it Al," responded the President trying immediately to take the level of the meeting to an informal one and to personalise the proceedings, "you're trying to sell back to the Chinese - in some sort of grand contra deal - something you don't own. You don't "own" the outputs of the University and you certainly don't own Mr Kemp's part of it, isn't that right Mr Kemp?"

The Englishman had already begun to feel extremely uncomfortable in this very American meeting, especially because of the aggressive tone of it and its atmosphere which was thick and tense. He coughed nervously before answering.

"There is an even more fundamental problem from our perspective," he responded tentatively. "We never did intend to monetise any benefit to us. It has been my ambition for many years to find a solution to mankind's energy crisis on this planet. We already have too many people with too many demands for energy that takes us beyond what we can provide. And with tens of thousands more people emerging from poverty and entering the world of consumerism every day, and with more and more people on the planet, this is a challenge of global consequence and of monumental importance to our species. This is something way beyond the issue of money - or politics. So our plan has always been to give the outputs of our endeavours freely to the market."

"I am not sure you'll be able to do that," Max Trueman intervened, smiling at Brian Kemp as he spoke though his eyes remained cold and steely. "The havoc you'd cause on the world's markets would be catastrophic. That is - assuming what you say you have you really do have."

"I find that very insulting," responded Kemp, beginning to forget the discomfort of the occasion and now feeling threatened by this American industrialist who was so full of his own importance. "What we have developed as an alternative fuel is beyond being questioned by people who do not know about such things". He fired this deliberate shot of aggression at Trueman who he hadn't liked from the outset of the meeting and who was growing in his mind as a major agitation. "And of course we've looked at mechanisms by which we can introduce this to the world in a way that doesn't cause markets to crash."

Trueman was about to say something else when Kemp continued.

"And, of course, if I may be allowed the opportunity to point this out, what the President is saying assumes the State of California has the rights of access and ownership to what we and the University have produced to - as it were - sell to the Chinese. The State of California has no such access. Indeed, I first came here on this visit to raise the issue with the Governor. He's assuming we would wish to sell our part of the solution. Let me make it very clear to everyone. We do not wish to do that. It is utterly against the fundamental principles upon which we've been operating for years as we've strived to develop this new fuel."

"But we believe it does," responded the Governor directly back to Kemp. "We would not have progressed this far without checking first. Our belief is that ultimately the State has all rights to products from the University as the University is an integral part of the State. Our Governance experts have advised us and that is how we've been dealing with the offer that has been brought to our table."

"But that can't include our element of it." Kemp was clearly very agitated now.

"Ironically you're shooting yourself in the foot," replied the Governor cuttingly with a renewed hardness in his voice. "Because of your charitable and benevolent instincts you say you don't want any return for taking your product to the market and you want open access to it. That maybe very laudable and the benevolence is to be applauded. But it also makes your involvement in this discussion - to be brutal but practical - somewhat null and void. We can now access your input via the knowledge the University has - as anyone can if you truly mean this to be available to the global community in the spirit of open access - and anyway, if you really get down to the nub of it, the University belongs to us."

"I don't believe you've got this right," Sue Williamson retorted. "Within the University the IP of any development lies with those who have invented it."

"That may be as you see it, Sue. It's not the way we do and not the way I've been advised. If you want to argue the detail you can do so with my legal team. And in any case, this whole issue of ownership is a red herring if you push me to become tough. I don't want to argue with you and the University. But if I have to I will and I'll do so in the courts - or we will take steps to reduce the amount of State support to the University. Or we'll do both. Don't forget Sue the level of State investment in this establishment - year on year. I don't mind how we do this but I'll make it clear to you right now, this is something we will win. I have to win."

"But Washington will veto this," the President spoke for the first time for a while. "We can't let you do this Al."

"I'm sorry Mr President," the Governor carefully elected not to go to a Christian name basis though the two had known each other for years. "The same applies to you. The deal is too good for us. If you try and veto me we'll take Washington to the Courts. And that'll take ages - years maybe. And while that's happening we'll see the deal progress anyway. And what'll you do to try and stop me? Arrest me? Send troops in to stop us? Bomb our oil storage depots? What'll you do Mr President?" Al Williams spat the challenge out.

"I'll see you in the courts Al." barked back the President. And with that he stormed out.

Chapter 10

If he cared to open his eyes he would have seen nothing but damp pavement. But Bond lay as flat as he could to the wet concrete, partly underneath the body of his Georgian friend, head down and eyes tightly shut.

They had crashed together onto the pavement as the car sped towards them. Bond could hear tyres on wet tarmac and the roaring engine as it closed in on them. He could also hear gunfire, some a short distance away, some next to him. Sharp, short bursts of fire came from the direction of the approaching car, then ear splitting explosions from whatever weapon Georgi close by Bond's right ear. Georgi fired three or four times - Bond wasn't sure. He certainly wasn't counting. He could smell the cordite. It made his eyes sting though he thought they were fully shut. He felt a tug and a quick stab of pain in his left shoulder as the night filled with another sound - the agonised screams of tyres under massive stress as the oncoming car lost control. Bond gained enough confidence to raise his head a little and open his eyes. The car approaching fast from his left, gunman firing from the open rear window, now veered onto the opposite pavement and sideswiped a wall in a mighty crash and spray of metallic sparks before returning to the road in a far from controlled fashion. It swerved past them and continued on its way in a series of lurches before disappearing into the night.

"Stay where you are." Georgi commanded. He rose swiftly and ran from where he had been lying against Bond and in the direction the taxi had gone. Bond watched from his still prone position. Only a couple of minutes passed before Georgi was back and helping Bond to his feet.

"Amateurs!" he grunted at Bond. "And thank your God for that. If they had been pros we wouldn't be alive now."

"What the hell was that all about?" asked Bond. "Were they after me? The Scottish police warned me I was in danger. Is that what that was about? Who were they? How come you fired back? How come you've got a gun? And how did you know? How did you know that was going to happen before it did? You threw me to the floor before they'd even fired at us. I thought it was the bloody taxi not a load of assassins."

"So many questions my friend - so much talk - so many words. I think it's a reaction. You're in shock," replied Georgi, now taking a close look at Bond's left shoulder. "And you've been hit. Not badly. But you've been hit. I think it's just grazed you but we need to take a look at it as soon as we can. First we need to get out of here before anyone starts to get curious or the police arrive."

With Georgi's help Bond walked with his friend away from the scene. His legs felt like rubber and he could feel his whole body weight. He wasn't sure whether it was a result of too much vodka and beer, loss of blood, sheer terror or a combination of them all. The road was badly lit and he remained scared and alert as to what else might happen. He was relieved when, after less than five minutes walking, they reached a more major road with better street lighting and busy passing traffic despite it still being very early in the morning. Bond felt less vulnerable here. With cabs few and far between at this extremely early hour, Georgi used his mobile phone to call up another taxi and they were both delighted and relieved when it arrived in next to no time - and this time it was the genuine article.

Georgi's 'small town apartment' turned out to be just a short walk from the historic and infamous Prospect of Whitby inn. Bond hadn't been there for years, not since younger days when he was fostering a rebel image and thought if the inn was good enough to be frequented by people such as Dickens, Pepys, Whistler and Turner, it was good enough for him. Georgi's apartment at Wapping Wall, just down the still cobblestoned road from the Dickensian inn, was originally part of the old spice warehouses, enormous riverside buildings which 250 years before housed and processed the spices brought from far flung places by the clipper ships. They had been turned into apartments some 30 years ago. The front door to Georgi's led immediately to a wide staircase up which Bond staggered with help from Georgi to an enormous lounge with a picture window filling the far wall. The panoramic view of the Thames was spectacular with Tower Bridge to the right. The dawning day showed promise of being a bright one and the river was already lively, the water glistening but generally blue in reflection of a more or less cloud free sky.

There were two major surprises for Bond. Firstly, it was immediately apparent to him that this was luxurious living despite how Georgi had described it at the Russian Club. It indicated quite clearly that his Georgian friend was doing very well from his new role in life.

The second surprise came from the bedroom and into the lounge and was nearly six feet of staggeringly sensual femininity with hazel hair and brown eyes. The woman wore a brightly coloured full length silk gown in red and yellow patterns with depictions of large flower heads. The thin flowing garment was tied casually at the waist by a band. Above and below the band its effectiveness in keeping the two halves of the gown together was questionable as gaps frequently appeared offering the briefest of glimpses of the nakedness that lay beneath. And those legs! Bond would have died for those legs that seemed to extend for ever and were shaped fit for a Goddess. In fact, the whole vista was, thought Bond, from another world.

"This is Nagriza," said Georgi casually, helping Bond take his coat off to reveal a blood soaked jacket and shirt. The girl came quickly to Bond's side and helped take off his jacket and shirt. Both she and Georgi examined what was almost just a graze but with a little depth to it.

"It's a clean wound," said the girl who spoke English but with a heavy accent - maybe Eastern European thought Bond. Maybe Georgian perhaps.

The two of them busied themselves in dressing the wound, first cleaning it with an antiseptic liquid then strapping a pad across the cut. Both his helpers, thought Bond, knew what they were doing. It had the deft touch of experts. These two knew how to dress battle wounds.

"It seemed to me you knew that was going to happen - before it happened," said Bond, patched up and now enjoying a very large mug of coffee. "Were you lucky or had you had some sort of premonition or sixth sense?"

"What do you mean?" asked Georgi.

"You threw me to the ground before anything happened," said Bond.

"You are wrong, my friend," Georgi responded. "I see things you do not see. As we came out of the Russian Club someone flashed a torch. It was to my right so I guess you maybe wouldn't have seen it. It must have been a signal to the car driver but - you are right perhaps - it was like a sixth sense signal to me which is why I threw you onto the floor. That's what I went to see after the car had gone. I went to see if I could find the person with the torch. But nobody was there."

"And how the hell have you got a gun?"

"Are, well. There you are my friend. My 007 friend. You have found me out."

Bond winced at the 007 reference.

"Look Georgi. You know what I think about my name. It's an embarrassment and an encumbrance. My life and that of my fictitious namesake are about as far removed as they could be - and, to be very honest, that's the way I prefer it. Georgi - I don't like being shot at!"

Georgi winked at him in fun. "Maybe your world and that of 007 have got closer!" he said.

"What do you mean?" asked Bond. "Stop pissing about Georgi. I seem to have been pulled into something that has nothing to do with me - nothing in line with my life at all. But I have walked into a triple murder in Scotland and now I've been shot at in London. I'm warned my life is possibly in danger. And I get shot at. This is not funny!"

"No it's not," replied his friend. "But I do see a funny side to it. It must be my Georgian sense of humour. Big difference to yours! But by some freaky coincidence - call of the Gods - throw of the dice - we seem - you and I – my drinking friend and confidante - to have got ourselves a common enemy. Not that I think they were behind tonight's attack. No, that was not professional. It was clumsy. The people you and I are up against are too good for that. Tonight was about something else. My guess is I was the target tonight, not you. If they had been good, we would not be here now. Or at best, you wouldn't. Tonight they were not good - hired kids probably - hired by one of the gangs I have been trying to break up."

"What the bloody hell are you talking about?" quizzed Bond. His friend was talking in riddles. "And Nagriza! Now here's another new surprise. You do play lots of things close to your chest Georgi."

His Georgian friend thought a while before responding.

"You are right," he eventually confessed. "I have - as you English sometimes so politically call it - been disingenuous with the actuality! I have not been fully truthful to you. But as we now seem to be fighting the same people, I'll tell you all about it. But this is between you and me. Together we can win this. So I need to trust you. Nagriza needs to trust you. I know we can because our friendship is long and deep. It is tied together with much Caucasus brandy!" Georgi laughed, then became serious again. "So I'll tell you the full story."

Chapter 11

Sum Taeyoung was taking stock again of how his scheme - the chess game - was progressing. All in all he felt well pleased with himself. In between reflecting on this and reading reports off his computer screen, he gazed at intervals through the window of his office at the wide expanse of the Ham River that today looked grey and flat, matching the colour and disposition of Seoul as it passed through the great sprawling metropolis.

The news was promising. Jo Summers and Chan Yung reported progress that was substantiated by news from various American media channels. It was not that difficult to track. Headlines across the daily press and television newscasts throughout America could not get away from the subject that was the hottest topic in that country and now repeated throughout the world's media. And the news from China was also encouraging for Sum. All in all, the plot was heading in just the direction he wanted.

Jo and Chan had reported on the meeting between the President, the Governor, the University's Chancellor and the Englishman Kemp. It seemed to have achieved what he had wanted. There was clearly great and increasing antagonism and tension between the President and the Governor and the Governor's threat to the Chancellor on funding issues had been a bombshell to everyone and an added bonus to Sum. He had not expected that. The threat that the State would withdraw support was extraordinary and an indication of the position the Governor was in. He was pulling tricks out of the bag like a cornered man fighting for survival.

The Chancellor had immediately called in her advisors who had confirmed that constitutionally the Governor could not do what he threatened to do. The State had no equity hold on the University that precluded the University managing its own affairs. But, whilst that was legally true, it was drawn to the Chancellor's attention that if the Governor cared to withdraw funding from the University the impact would be enormous - potentially devastating. It was, therefore, a threat the Chancellor could not ignore.

Predictably, the Englishman Kemp had returned home and consulted with his team of lawyers. But to Kemp's utter frustration and dismay, there was universal agreement that Kemp was poleaxed by his own philosophical and benevolent principles. The fact that he wanted to make his new fuel freely available to the global community outflanked any principles of Intellectual Property protection. In other words, he could not have an open source philosophy and protect his own rights. The two were diametrically opposed.

In the aftermath of the meeting at the University, Governor Williams had immediately hit the California media with a campaign of news articles and TV appearances justifying his rejection of the President's National Energy Plan. And it quickly became clear in response to this well orchestrated activity that the population of California was mostly in support of their local leader.

In the weeks that followed this campaigning activity intensified and counter noises started coming from the White House in a veritable avalanche that from a Californian perspective served only to agitate the differences. The President talked in emotional language about the Californian Governor's "betrayal of the Federation - the betrayal of those who died in the formation of the Constitution."

The more vitriolic the President's language became the more the citizens of California moved toward the idea of a breakaway. Governor Williams called his closest Commissioners and Senior Advisors to a battle plan meeting at his offices in Sacramento.

"It's becoming a real son of a bitch," the Governor told them. "There's more writs flying around my office than arrows were flying around the Little Big Horn!"

And the group pondered the volume of challenges coming out of the White House which was not insignificant. Finally Al Williams got something stuck in his head that became the basis of their deliberations.

"I remember," he told them, "when this big balled Rhodesian took on the British when the Brits still had an empire, though it was in its twilight years. There was a mighty battle as the Rhodesian Prime Minister, Ian Smith, demanded independence from Britain. When they refused he eventually made what became his famous - or was it infamous - Unilateral Declaration of Independence speech - UDI. It was an audacious act and it sparked an enormous political row. It became a protracted and damaging campaign, damaging to both sides. And with the UN and other major nations refusing to acknowledge Smith's call as being anything but illegal, Smith became isolated with just a few friends - like South Africa, for instance, backing him."

Marcus Alworth, Senior Advisor on Political Governance, looked worried, was worried and could not disguise the fact in what he said and how he said it.

"Al, Smith might have thought UDI was a good tactic. But it didn't work. He was screwed the minute the UN rejected it."

"I don't agree," argued the Governor. "Smith might not have got what he wanted when he wanted it and how he wanted it. Remember, he was running a white government in Africa, of all places. It's hardly surprising he wasn't globally popular! And this was the first move by a country within the British Empire to seek independence. He certainly wasn't running a campaign to win friends! So he was in unchartered waters. So are we. But history shows what he wanted to happen happened anyway - eventually, and maybe not as Smith hoped for. But Rhodesia got its independence and became Zimbabwe."

"But," joined in Dick Jefferson from the Governor's policy team and obviously expressing concerns felt by others in the group "we've got the

Constitution to overcome. Smith was in a very different place to us. He doesn't set precedence for us, Governor, or even offer a good example."

"I agree there's a lot of differences," responded Al Williams. "But the Rhodesian story maybe provides us with some sort of pathway. And anyway, in terms of the Constitution, you've been exploring that Marcus. Where have you got to?"

Alworth opened his brief case and took out some papers which he used to prompt his reply.

"Article IV, Section 3, Clause 1 of the Constitution says: *'New States may be admitted by the Congress into this Union but no new State shall be formed or erected within the Jurisdiction of any other State nor any State be formed by the Junction of two or more States, or Parts of States, without the Consent of the Legislatures of the States concerned as well as of the Congress'.* In my mind - and I have taken guidance on this - you could say that if Congress has the power to admit states to the Union and, further, has the power to create a state from an existing state or states with the permission of the state or states involved, then it follows that Congress has the power to remove a state from the Union with the permission of the state involved."

"But Congress isn't seeking to remove California from the Union," stressed the Governor. "We are."

"Of course," continued Alworth. "But in the 10th Amendment it says *'The powers not delegated to the United States by the Constitution, nor prohibited by it to the States, are reserved to the States respectively, or to the people.'*

Alworth looked up from his papers. "And that suggests there is clarity missing in the Constitution. It suggests to me that when a state is involved in something such as removal from the Union, if it has approved the idea of being out of the Union with its people, that ought to be sufficient."

"So, what does that really mean?" asked Masters.

"I think it means that if the Legislature of California asks to withdraw from the United States - and it has the proven will of the people behind it - Congress would have to approve, and a legal agreement between us and them would seal it."

"That means we're secure," said Harry Kutner, another policy advisor, but it was more a question than a statement.

The Governor responded. "I certainly think so. It looks strong. Obviously the White House won't agree and we've a long way to go on negotiations. It's clear in my mind there's a way forward for us but two things are essential. We must have a mandate from the people of California to do this and it would be more than helpful if we could encourage the UN onto our side. There is a narrow line between hostile secession - which is what Ian Smith tried to do with Rhodesia - and separation. Smith was accused of treason. We could be also. But not if we pursue a course of separation via a process of negotiation - with our people behind us."

This became the basis for the Governor's 'battle plan'. Whilst they continued to fight off a barrage of threats from Washington, the Governor declared to the media that he intended to give the people of California the democratic opportunity to "settle this one way or another" – with a state-wide referendum.

"Let the people speak," he proclaimed. It would ask three questions of the 25 million or so Californians eligible to vote.

1. Do Californians support the Governor's energy plan?
2. Do Californians favour the President's energy plan?
3. Would Californians support a move for the State to become independent?

When he got to see a copy of the document, the final question delighted Sum. His clients would also be pleased. Sum was also relieved that so far nothing had backfired from China. This, and pulling appropriate strings within the UN, had been by far the trickiest part of the plot. He had been worried all along about the Chinese side of the scheme which held many of the key ingredients and had taken much cunning, resolve and money to achieve. It was considerably aided in its execution by Sum's detailed knowledge of the workings of China's massive bureaucratic administrative machinery which left it ripe and vulnerable for fostering confusion and disarray, especially when liberal helpings of bribery were injected into the equation.

So, with the help of corrupt officials, the formation of a small, new specialist procurement unit of the Chinese Government focussed on buying oil for a "special project" of the Chinese Government, had gone ahead some time ago without raising any questions in the 'Zhongnanhai' of Beijing. Sum called it Asian Pacific Trading Inc. To all intents and purpose it looked like an official Chinese agency. The only main difference between perceptions and reality was that the specialist procurement unit was not a Government unit at all but something totally controlled by SDBI, funded by secret sources known only to Sum and surrounded by many smoke screens. It was something even the Chinese Governmental hierarchy missed. It was there. Nobody deemed it necessary to question its existence or what it was doing.

Under the pretext of acquiring oil for special Chinese projects, the unit started siphoning off quantities of oil purchased from Iraq, Qatar, and various other states which, largely, did not mind who they were selling oil to so long as the price was right and the money secure. In fact, as far as they were concerned, they were still selling oil to China, as they had before. In the eyes of the sellers, nothing had changed, only the address and details of the acquisition agency and the destination to where the purchased goods would be delivered. So Sum's special unit started storing large quantities of oil, enough to eventually respond to a Californian deal once the deal had been made. Enough to, at least, start the process if he needed to. He certainly didn't want more than that.

And now, as Sum viewed the array of reports before him, California had backed its Governor. Of all the actions within Sum's complex plot, this was the only one over which he had little or no control. Whilst the Governor and his team remained blissfully unaware of the strings Sum was pulling - in China, in the UN and elsewhere - to orchestrate events to match his plan and its timetable, the one imponderable element of the plot had been the referendum. Now that was in the bag, much to Sum's relief, and achieved in the face of mounting threats from the White House including court actions, financial penalties, and various sanctions. By an overwhelming majority, the citizens of California rejected the US National Fuel Plan and gave a clear mandate to the Governor to pursue his own oil acquisition programme. There had been a growing sea of opinion that Californians were disillusioned by a continuing state of affairs in which they gave far more to the Federal Government than they received back, and the President's National Fuel Plan had compounded that.

And, to the horror of the White House, the dismay of the President and the delight and triumph of Sum, the referendum gave a clear view that a majority of Californians saw the moment was right to now go their own way as potentially one of the richest nations of the world, potentially the ninth biggest economy on the planet, to free itself from the encumbrances of a distanced national administration, to stop subsidising poorer States in the Union, and to enable itself to control its own destiny. It was a significant and historic vote of confidence in the Governor, a slap in the face for the President, and pure joy to Sum. In addition, across the United States the top topic was California's move to independence. In Texas, the movement for independence there was fuelled and reinvigorated by the happenings in its neighbouring State.

Rumblings in other southern States were getting louder while the northern part of the country rallied round the President. The North/South divide was the stuff of headlines and many observers felt obliged to dig up history and look back to the times of the Civil War.

Uncertainty was rife across the country and provided an ideal platform for anti-establishment factions to become very vocal.

Fear was running rife through the White House, reaching fever pitch when in his latest round of newspaper and TV interviews, Governor Williams declared his next move.

"Given this historic and clear mandate from the people of California, I have met with the leaders of the United Nations. Their response has been fantastic and their support highly practical and gratefully appreciated. They, as I, believe we have been through a right and proper democratic process. Our rights as a State within the Federation - and, indeed, the rights of the Federation itself - are clouded in a constitution born out of the chaos of our Civil War. We cannot find any reason why, by law, we cannot take forward the actions we now plan."

"We therefore intend to declare to the family of nations that constitute the United Nations Assembly, a Unilateral Declaration of Independence for the State of California. We have consulted with the UN throughout the development of this situation and its officers are now looking for a suitable opportunity in their agenda to help us formulate - then declare - a Unilateral Declaration. For reasons of our own security and especially our energy negotiations, I hope we will be able to achieve this much sooner than later."

Sum's plot for his clients was progressing at a pace almost beyond belief. But the real play of the chess pieces, known only to Sum and his clients, was yet to come.

Chapter 12

In Georgi's apartment they had moved on from the hot coffee to something to try and tackle the aftermath of the alcohol. Bond in particular had a pounding head though he failed to discern whether it was attributable to the vodka and beer mix, to the excitement that had followed, or a combination of both. So they had looked to a traditional cure but one with new, state of the art modifications. This was a Georgi special, a homemade version of Kvass which Nagriza made not only from the traditional black rye bread, herbs, tomatoes and mint, but with anything else she cared to throw in at the creative stage of making it. Her version depended upon what she could find in Georgi's cupboards and fridge.

"After the war with Russia," said Georgi. "What I told you was true - at least it was to start with. I did get a job with a department of the European Union that was looking after the new accession states, the former countries of the Soviet Union now entering or seeking to enter the EU. Through that I saw an opportunity and I left to become a freelance specialising in issues to do with intellectual property. It was interesting stuff and not badly paid."

"I did that for a couple of years before an old friend of mine approached me. It took a while and several meetings to understand why he wanted to see me. Eventually he was happy enough to open up and put on the table an offer for me to become part of the European Secret Service."

"I didn't know there was such a thing," interrupted Bond.

"There isn't - officially that is," continued Georgi. "It's sort of morphed into being - created itself virtually by accident initially as other units were formed - the European Satellite Centre, the Intelligence Division and the Joint Situation Centre. It didn't take much to extract bits off each of them and form something called the EU Intelligence Service which even most Members of the European Parliament don't know exists."

"Anyway, it does. Its communications base is here in London. I almost live on the premises. I'll show you later."

"My first assignment was to investigate the strange story of the disappearance of a young man from an island off the North coast of Scotland. He was involved with a project that made hydrogen from wind generated energy. Amazing really. The islanders were frustrated by being at the end of the energy supply line and suffering frequent power black outs. So, being a particularly clever and inventive lot, they built themselves a couple of wind turbines. One of the problems of generating energy from wind is what to do with energy the turbines produce when you don't have an immediate use for it. They started mucking about with hydrogen, working with a chap called Brian Kemp from England who was doing something very similar. Together they formulated this methodology of converting the excess energy into hydrogen which they could then store. In fact, the islanders had their own small car powered by hydrogen."

"Amazingly, considering we're talking about a tiny lump of land in the North Sea, this was one of the first - if not the first - car anywhere in the UK that was licensed for road use but powered by hydrogen as a fuel. Incredible really - on a small island off the north coast of Scotland, of all places!"

"From this small beginning they formed their own company .The chap who disappeared was one of those who inspired the project - and he was now seeking to sell the technology they had developed to other community groups - anywhere and not just in the UK. The project gained a lot of publicity and visibility. Our man became used to treading the corridors of Whitehall and Brussels. Then he just disappeared. It was all very strange and became the subject of an extensive police investigation."

"I was asked to sort of poke around the story a bit. The missing guy had been born on the island, was as familiar with living in such a place as anyone, knew every inch of the island like the native he was, and had no reason not to continue what seems to have been a fulfilling life. But he just disappeared. Like a magic act.

There one minute. Then puff - gone the next. There was no logic to it, no sensible reasons, no clues and no trace. Not even any suggestion the chap intended to leave the island. He left his home to go to work - 100 meters away - and didn't arrive anywhere. Certainly his family hadn't expected him to go anywhere."

"It was while I was delving into that story that I found the missing chap had just started dealing with an organisation called Asian Pacific Trading Inc. – APTI."

"Really!" exclaimed Bond. "APTI!"

"Yes," continued Georgi. "Using my experience in European IP as a cover, I delved into APTI. It has all the looks of being a Chinese Government procurement agency. That's what it says it is. That's what most people take it to be - including - amazingly - the Chinese Government. But I think that somehow it's connected to another company - not Chinese but South Korean - called Sustainable Development Broking International - or SDBI. Not many people know about this connection and we're still searching into it."

"I got quite involved with SDBI at one stage and even had a meeting booked with one of its founders, an Anglicised South Korean called Sum Taeyoung. He's ex the LSE and Harvard. And that says a lot. He's clever. No doubt about that. And cunning. I never did meet him and I became very suspicious of both him and the SDBI outfit. Though they run a legitimate business, I also found they run a very secretive side too. They use their international consultancy and trading as a disguise for their true reason for existing. Sum Taeyoung - I believe but can't prove it yet - makes a lot of his money running weapons and drugs and from sophisticated forms of international sabotage. He orchestrates social upheaval which gives him the markets he wants in which to make money."

"I never did find anything to resolve the mystery of the guy missing on the Scottish island but it did introduce SDBI into my life. I was never able to prove anything but I believe to this day that the Scottish energy expert had seen behind the facade of APTI - maybe even traced it like I did to SDBI, and found its darker side and paid the penalty. I hadn't heard of them before encountering them via this Scottish mystery."

"It was around this time it became apparent I wasn't the only person delving into SDBI. Several agencies were - and still are. And because they were all secret agencies, not one of them knew that others were looking too - except me. One of the benefits of working for the European Secret Service is the strength of its intelligence. It sometimes gives you a unique overview. We knew the Americans, Russians and some others were all sniffing round SDBI. One agency was the SNB, better known as the Uzbekistan National Secret Service. Uzbekistan had been approached by APTI. I think they were investigating the possibility of getting oil out of the Bukhara-Khiva region. The Uzbekistan government asked us to do a check on APTI which was how I got involved and how I found the link to SDBI. But they also had one of their own agents on the case. The agent was a lady. And now you've met her!"

Georgi waved an extravagant gesture towards Nagriza.

"Allow me the pleasure of formerly introducing you to Nagriza Karimov, formerly of the SNB and now working with me."

Nagriza stood and mockingly bowed in response to the introduction, the movement opening the gap in the front of her loose gown so Bond caught a clear and not at all fleeting view of the origins of the delightful shapes that had been so evident from the moment Nagriza had walked into the room. Despite the pain from his shoulder, his fatigue, the aftermath of the alcohol, Bond could not control the testosterone reaction he could feel in his groin. This was, he again said to himself, one hell of a woman.

"God almighty Georgi," Bond said. "This is some bloody story."

Georgi shrugged his shoulders as if to say it was all a bit matter of fact and continued. "Not long ago I found APTI is involved with activity in America. I - er, we - have not yet found out in detail what they're doing there and we sort of pulled back a bit when I was taken off the work because it was felt my cover had been blown."

"We know it's something about brokering a deal on oil between China and California - and that has stimulated a Californian threat to break away from the Federation. You must have seen the media coverage. The deal that's fired this all off seems to be an exchange in which China gives California oil in return for access to some new hi-technology which purports to be a radical answer to the world's declining oil situation. We don't know the detail and it's all a bit of a puzzle. For instance, how come China is giving away oil when it's got growing dependencies for the stuff? It already has to import oil from wherever it can get it, like Central Asia, Russia, Venezuela, Iran, Indonesia - and elsewhere in the Middle East. It doesn't produce anywhere near enough to satisfy its own needs. And those needs are rocketing. So how come it can be giving oil away? It seems plain crazy."

"But we know there is this clandestine side to APTI - SDBI - so I believe there is more to this than meets the eye. Much more."

"And I think I'm now known to the darker side of SDBI and I don't think I'm that popular. So when you mentioned APTI I was more than a little interested."

"So, now, my friend, you've heard my story. Now tell us yours. How have you got involved? What's driven you to get into this mess?"

Bond thought for a while. Nagriza moved to where Georgi was sitting on a couch, stretched out on the floor in a lounging position with her head on his lap. Georgi gently caressed her hazel hair. Bond wondered about their relationship. It was clearly beyond just a professional working one. He felt an uncontrollable and irrational sense of jealousy.

"It's difficult to know where to start," sighed Bond. "And what you've just told me. I'm having difficulty taking all that on board. It's a crazy story. I seem to have been sucked into a living nightmare. It's taking some time to get used to it."

There was another long pause as he gathered his thoughts together.

"This is going to sound sloppy," he said in a resigned fashion. "And a bit futile, maybe. I'm almost fed up of repeating this - of hearing my own plaintiff pleas."

"Try me," encouraged his friend.

"OK - it goes something like this.

"There's all sorts of ways of expressing this. For instance, there's the principles of the biosphere. Do you know about the biosphere?"

There were negative responses from both Georgi and Nagriza though Nagriza did mutter something about a bubble. But it was without much conviction. Bond took it as a more or less 'no'.

"We" he started, still wondering how to deliver this message with real conviction. "The human species and every other living matter - live in a biosphere. And yes, Nagriza, you're basically right. It's a sort of bubble. What's in the biosphere is pretty well all there is for us to live on - air, water, food, the land on which to grow our food, fish in the sea, minerals to mine, all other living species and so on. There is nothing else outside the bubble - except the power of the sun and the occasional extra terrestrial lump that hits us. But in terms of resources, what we have is what we have. There is no more."

"Everything in the biosphere interlinks one way or another. Some links are obvious. Some less so and are quite tenuous. It's the most sophisticated, complex and delicately balanced world we know to exist. We now know an amazing amount about the space in which our planet is located. And we know a lot about other planets we can see. Scientific exploration is now reaching so far out it is on the fringes of when time began. Yet we have not found a planet anything like Planet Earth. As far as we know, it's unique. With the billions of billions of planets out there, the odds must be that somewhere there's something similar. But as of the moment, Planet Earth is like nowhere else. And everything that makes it tick is contained within the bubble, apart from the exceptions I've mentioned. But the interdependency of everything within the bubble is paramount and in many instances that linkage is quite fragile."

"So, into that highly complex, highly sophisticated, often delicate, - unique on an intergalactic scale - biosphere you inject a species that is massively dominant, which uses the 'assets' within the biosphere without consideration as to what happens when all those assets have gone or have at least been hugely damaged, and without much appreciation or seeming care for how its actions impact on everything else in the biosphere."

"Of course that dominant species is us and we are creating havoc. If we don't better control our actions then ultimately the biosphere will become unstable and start to die. The irony is, of course, that we are also dependent upon the biosphere being maintained in a stable state. If the biosphere becomes unstable, our own position becomes untenable. With me so far?"

Nagriza and Georgi both nodded their confirmation.

"Already," continued Bond, "species within the biosphere are dying at an alarming and accelerating pace because of the actions of we humans. I find it more than worrying. It frightens me. And it horrifies me that we, as the dominant and allegedly intelligent species, are acting so irresponsibly. That might sound a bit pompous but we do have responsibilities as the dominant species but we also have responsibilities for our own sustainability on this planet. Currently we are compromising both."

Nagriza interrupted. "Didn't I read somewhere that we might be destroying things we haven't even discovered yet - like microbes and plants? And that some of these might potentially have provided solutions to some of our medical problems."

"I believe we know more about space than we know about our own seas," replied Bond, "which are largely unexplored at any great depths. Every time there's a record breaking dive we discover new species. So we don't know what's down there. And when you think of how much of our medication is based on other life forms - from microbes upwards - who knows what solutions have yet to be discovered. That is, unless we destroy what could have proved helpful before we even discover it."

"But to go back to the biosphere, I think we human beings are like a species that's on a course of self destruction - species suicide. A lot of people are talking about how we need to save the planet. What concerns me is not about saving the planet. I'm totally convinced the planet will survive. We may seriously screw it up. But it'll survive us like it's survived other species that have been and gone before, like other disasters it's encountered in its long history. The only difference with us is we can seriously harm the world in which we live - way beyond anything any other species has ever done. Even now, with all we know, we are throwing obnoxious gases into the atmosphere in enormous quantities and I, for one, can't believe that's not impacting on our climate. There's still much debate as to whether or not we're damaging the climate or whether climate change is just a natural phenomenon - a cycle."

"My attitude is, dare we take it for granted we're not having an impact? If we aren't, fair enough. Well, not really. My gut instincts tell me it's wrong to be discarding the huge volumes of stuff we send up into the atmosphere. It's just got to be harmful. But let's assume the ultimate answer is that we are contributing to a change in the way our climate behaves. If we wait much longer to do anything about it - and just continue to debate whether it's right or wrong but don't do anything - we are likely to pass a point where recovery is possible. I'd hate to be counted amongst those who voted to do nothing! What a responsibility! But as I see it, we may be beyond a point of retrieval anyway. The damage we've done is, I believe, causing climate change to happen now and we'll have to live with the consequences - which are likely to grow and grow."

"The clever thing would be to stop doing what has already caused damage. But we don't. For instance, the scientific fraternity tells us we must stop building coal fired energy plants that are contributing to global warming. The world political community says it's trying to stop global warming exceeding 2 degrees. But scientists say we are already on track for 4 degrees warming. Five degrees, they tell us, would be catastrophic - would be a calamity for the biosphere. Yet today, around the world, we're building 1300 coal fired power stations! Does that sound like the action of a responsible species?"

"1300 coal fired power stations?" queried Georgi.

"If I remember right," replied Bond, "an organisation called the Global Warming Policy Foundation reckons China and India are commissioning four new coal-fired power stations ever week."

"Jesus!" grunted Georgi.

"And that's despite knowing what damage we might potentially cause the planet," continued Bond. "Which might be to a level that ultimately wipes us out. I think the planet itself will eventually self-repair from whatever we might do to it. However, I think we're eventually bound to fade from the scene. We will sort of self-destruct. Hundreds of other species have done so before and so have many other civilisations. I try - very hard - to be positive but the more I get involved the more concerned I get."

"Basically I think we've created a set of global challenges that we can't respond to with any effect because the management structures we've got are incapable of doing so. The challenges we face are global. Our civilisation is managed not on a global basis but locally, whether that's nationally or in geographical zones like the EU. We've no single global management structure. There's no single command structure to take unilateral decisions and actions. Instead what we have is a highly complex global society that we try to run through local structures - governments. But they exist to look after their local populations. That's who votes them into power. Anything that's of a more global nature causes them to struggle and often they come into conflict in an unanswerable battle between local interests and global ones. That, to me, is one of the reasons why the UN has proved inadequate in responding."

"Into that you have to sprinkle cultural differences and religion. So asking the global community to act in unison is virtually impossible."

"I think religion has much to answer for," Nagriza offered.

"I think you're right," agreed Bond. "But when people become trapped in poverty and can see no escape - no hope - at least religion is somewhere for them to retreat to. Sometimes. But when society drops into chaos and despair, and the disconnection between the people and the politicians who are supposed to manage their national affairs becomes wider, it provides the perfect environment for extremists - whether they're religious or political or just troublemakers - to recruit people into their ranks."

"We often demonstrate this amazing ability to act together in the face of enormous threats or in response to disasters once they've happened. But mainly only after they've happened. We tend to be reactive rather than proactive. Now we face what some people call 'The Perfect Storm' - a vibrant, boiling cocktail of problems that we've recognised for years, got amazingly sophisticated knowledge about, but singularly fail to do anything about collectively and on a world-wide scale."

"We've a global population that's the biggest the planet has had to cope with so far - around 6 billion. It's set to increase by 50% to 9 billion in just 35 years. The planet's never seen so many people or such growth in numbers at such a rate. We've tens of thousands of people leaving poverty to become consumers - joining a process of gobbling up what resources we have at an alarming rate and seemingly with little concern for the fact we can't replace most of them! We've surging growth in Brazil, India and China."

"The growth in China is staggering," reflected Georgi.

"Investment in infrastructure accounts for much of China's GDP," Bond said. "The country is said to have built the equivalent of Rome every two months in the past decade! Can you believe that? Did you know that in 2010 China poured more than half the concrete poured anywhere in the world! And with such a large pool of labour it's harder to put the brakes on when growth slows and supply outstrips demand."

"They've got seven to eight million people entering the workforce in China every single year, so they've got to give them something to do. To me it's an unsustainable equation. The growth of China is based on debt - the biggest pile of debt we've ever seen. Lehman Brothers was the first bank to crash in what became the global collapse of the banking system. But the debt China has accumulated makes that look like chicken feed. To me it's a growing bubble that I think will inevitably burst. I hate to think what will happen then. It's an alarming prospect."

"It's beyond my comprehension," said Nagriza. "I just can't grasp it. The numbers are just too big to think about."

"All this growth and huge numbers of new consumers is putting an enormous strain on what resources we have," continued Bond. "What we have is what we have. For years, WWF has called it 'One Planet Living' - living off what we have on this planet. But we're currently consuming stuff as if we have two and a half planets of resources. It's crazy! There is no more - until we go off to the moon and other planets and start mining and harvesting them. And, no doubt, we'll end up wrecking those planets too."

"And India is following China's lead. India plans to build five mega cities in the next five years along the Delhi-Mumbai industrial corridor alone. And then there's Brazil - and behind Brazil other South American countries that are trying to shake themselves out of their destitute past into consumer style societies based on Western style economies - which are based on growth and in recent years have demonstrated they don't work. The model might have been right once. It isn't now! It's redundant."

"Meanwhile we continue to pollute and to waste. Despite all the political rhetoric, we continue to do more of both - not less. It's incredulous! Beyond belief! And whether or not climate change relates directly to the way we're continuing to pollute now doesn't matter in some respects. As I said before, the damage has been done and climate change is happening."

Georgi joined in again. "I agree. I don't know whether it's because of climate change - and even if climate change is a cyclic characteristic of nature - or manmade - or both, but I do see around the world more flooding - more flash storms - and more droughts than ever before."

"Yes," agreed Bond. "And they're at severe and massively damaging levels. Severe events weren't that frequent not so long ago. Now we have a proliferation of them. They are becoming the norm. It seems ironic to me that while the agricultural crops of Europe are wiped out by unprecedented flooding, in the same year the bread basket of America is beset with the longest drought it's ever experienced. And in the same period, fire spreads across rural Eastern Russia. So global food stocks are badly hit - just when we've millions of more mouths to feed."

Bond paused and drank more Kvass.

"Alongside this we've had as I've already mentioned the biggest financial disaster witnessed by the world for generations. And to give you an example of how our political masters are responding to all of this, they jumped and reacted when the banks went bust and just wrote seemingly endless amounts of money. But when the economist Lord Stern told them they needed to spend just a fraction of that to respond to climate change, they didn't. I think that clearly shows where political priorities lie, in whichever country you happen to be. It seems we can find the money to save the banks but not find the money to respond to climate change. Unbelievable!"

"The reality is," said Georgi in a resigned voice. "The world is driven by money. Nothing else counts. Nobody cares about anything else. Money means power. It means comfort. And without it you're in trouble."

"I agree," said Bond. "And when it comes to environmental issues, officials from more than 250 countries, about 150 heads of state and nearly 20,000 people attended the Earth Summit in Rio. So many thousands went to the environmental conference in Copenhagen it nearly seized. Hundreds of thousands of people have spent untold amounts of money going to God knows how many events to talk about the problems we've got. But where is the resultant action? Virtually zilch! Despite all of this talk, all of the promises, all of the rhetoric, the World Business Council says it all adds up to hardly making a dent in making the world truly sustainable."

"And while all this goes on and we show amazing inability to do anything. Increasingly more numbers of people fall into poverty. Incredulously, a child dies from malnutrition somewhere on the planet every eight seconds. 18,000 die every day! In this modern world - when people like you and I live in such comfort and security! What sickening evidence of our lack of responsibility! Close on 100 million people don't have access to clean water. Would you believe there are more people on the planet with a mobile phone than there are people who have a toilet? It beggars belief. In this highly sophisticated, space age world! It's beyond disgrace."

"Now we have the impact of the collapse of financial stability. It's creating a situation where most welfare systems have lost their ability to protect household incomes and to be able to help the poor. The numbers of people starving on this planet in the 21st Century is just sickening."

"So, Georgi, I am amazed we haven't seen more social unrest by now. There's been smatterings of it but with people getting hungry, not being able to earn money and now not being able to buy fuel to keep families warm and dry, to me it's a recipe for anarchy. I'm absolutely astounded that we haven't had millions on the streets looking for the blood of their leaders who are so letting them down. It's a set of circumstances which gives opportunity on a plate to the radicals and anarchists. I'm amazed we have not seen the start of global revolution and a break down of society as we know it."

"I think what I do is pitiful, pathetic and puny. But at worst I shall go to my grave knowing I at least attempted to do something. And if it ultimately comes to a moment of final judgement, at least those making judgement will be able to say - "well, at least he tried!""

Bond sat back and stared at his friends, trying to judge their reaction. A cavernous, despairing silence dominated the three of them. Nothing happened for some minutes before Nagriza, speaking slowly and softly, said: "I know you're right. Lots of people know you're right. But I think one of the problems is that individuals see this as such an enormous problem they think there's nothing they can do that makes a meaningful impact. And they're just too busy surviving in their own little worlds. And they're precious about what they have - very protective. So they either do nothing, because they don't know what to do, or think that if they do anything it will be pretty futile, or they think their lifestyles will be threatened so they rebel against change, or they make their own gestures - like cycling rather than driving their cars, like eating less meat, like trying to be less wasteful. But it's such a little response to such a massive problem. It sometimes seems a waste of effort. People say 'what's the point of me doing anything when you've got countries like China polluting their cities and the planet.'"

Georgi had been deep in thought. "What has brought us together is a product of what you're talking about, Gene. Growing energy needs and the reduction in available resources is providing people who want to cause trouble an ideal opportunity. And that's what we are up against with Sum and his team. That's where we have a common battle front. Gene, I think the time has come, my friend, to show you more about how we are fighting back."

Chapter 13

"These rather nice places to live," said Georgi with the three of them standing by the picture window in the lounge with Tower Bridge not far from them on the right, "were developed from old warehouses. I think the one this apartment was part of used to do more than just store goods. I think it was also used to make a product - right here. It was mustard. At the back end of the 1800s, the clipper ships - big, fast ships with huge sailing rigs, loaded with spices and herbs from exotic parts of the world, unloaded here where the content was used to mix mustards and other products which were immediately loaded back onto the same ships for export."

"Eventually more modern docks, ships with engines and more modern manufacturing methods made these warehouses redundant and they stood for decades unwanted and unused. Then around the 1970s permission was granted for speculative developers to turn them into apartments. Which brings us to why we're able to stand here and look at this fantastic view."

"The Thames Barrier opened in 1982, around the same time as the warehouses started to be developed. But at the early stages of development there was great concern about the risk of flooding to these new developments, despite the barrier. The effectiveness of the barrier had yet to be proved. So basement areas in the warehouses weren't included in the conversion programme as the rest of the buildings were turned into modern apartments. Instead, they were sealed to try and ensure they didn't flood."

"Twenty years or so later, the barrier has proved itself and modern building technology has developed as well. So when it came to where to establish the communications centre for the new European Union Intelligent Service, though when it was formed its administration centre was opened in Brussels, political pressure and expediency led for it to be in London. Even the French had to concede that with GCHQ in Cheltenham - and its close links to the Americans - and MI5 and 6 in London, when it came to intelligence gathering the UK was more advanced than any other European state. So amongst those in Brussels who were involved - and there weren't many of them - it was agreed the Comms Centre for the new EUIS should be in London. And when looking for somewhere to put a team of people who don't officially exist, where better than in some space that also doesn't officially exist - like the basements of this warehouse. Come on. I'll show you."

They waited while Nagriza did a quick change of clothes, swapping the thin flowing materials of the robe she had been wearing for black jeans and a black sweatshirt which, Bond noted with inner satisfaction, had a deep cut front to it. Georgi walked toward a door Bond had noticed but not really noticed. It was simply another door. It matched others in the room but was no more or less than the rest. But though it had a gold coloured door knob the same as the others, it took an unexpected action to open it. Georgi pointed his watch face at the door and pressed a button on the watch. Momentarily nothing happened but then Bond became aware of the near silent hum of an electrical motor in action, then the sound of mechanisms in movement, and slowly the door opened revealing a well illuminated corridor.

"Impressive. My God, Georgi, you're full of surprises," said Bond. Georgi led Bond and Nagriza along a short corridor to a spiral staircase that headed steeply downwards. Pretence to elegance had been left in the apartment. Gone was the deep pile carpet, replaced now by roughly hewn stone and bare brickwork. It was quite a long downward journey during which a distinct dankness and coldness started to prevail. Eventually they confronted a steel door which was activated again by Georgi's watch. They passed through it and into a significantly sized room which showed its origins by again having unclad brick walls and a ceiling with exposed wooden beams. There were no windows and just two other doors. While the corridor and stairs had been cold with a damp feeling to them, here there was the distinct warmth and dryness of a modern building and effective h&v.

Three people, all sitting at work stations and surrounded by computer screens, looked up as the trio entered. Bond had already realised their arrival was no surprise. Around the wall hung several large screens and one showed images from a camera located on the staircase down which they had just come.

"Meet Jamie, Alan and Jane," said Georgi with a sweep of the arm in introduction to the three who nodded back in welcome.

"There are three ways out of here," said Georgi. "The one we've just come down, the door over there that leads to another apartment, and that door over there - which is our emergency exit - to be used only in moments of real stress and danger. The escape route itself is pretty dangerous and best used only at night. The passage from that door leads to another passageway which in turn leads to the tunnel that goes under the Thames to Rotherhithe. Historically it's famous because it was the first tunnel to be built under a navigable river. It goes back to before 1850 and was built by the famous engineer, Isambard Kingdom Brunel. He built it as a foot tunnel which would have been very good for us. Unfortunately for us most of its life it's been a train tunnel and today it has mainline trains running through it. As fewer trains run at night, if we're going to have an emergency and need to leave quickly, I hope it'll be at night!"

"The other benefit is that it links us to the other side of the river where M15 is located so if we want reinforcements we theoretically have another route by which we can get at them quickly - or they can get to us."

Georgi led them to a black glass topped table where they sat with a large computer screen before them.

"I concluded," Georgi continued to Bond who was finding it hard to come to terms with everything he was seeing and the environment in which he now was, "that it was time we took your fight - my fight - to the enemy."

Georgi clicked a hand control he had picked up from the table and the screen came to life. Bond found he was looking at the outside of a block of offices. He didn't recognise where it was. It could have been anywhere. It was modern, concrete, high rise, with big windows.

"Welcome to South Korea," announced Georgi. "To be more precise, welcome to Seoul. And to be even more precise, welcome to the HQ of Sustainable Development Brokers International." Georgi paused, obviously proud to be full of even more surprises for his friend. "And more importantly" - the image on the screen changed as the camera zoomed at speed closer and closer to one particular window in the building, then as if through it and into the room inside. Now the image was hazy and distorted but Bond could make out fixtures and furniture in the room.

"Bloody hell," was all he could say.

"You are, my dear friend, in the offices of no lesser person than Sum Taeyoung. We have talked about him before. Now you can see where he works."

Bond was amazed beyond words.

"And we can hear what's going on in the room too. The picture is distorted because what you are looking at are images that have been massively enhanced by an extremely powerful computer. We have penetrated some decorative net curtains that try and portray a feeling of innocence but which have anti-snooper characteristics built into them. And we've also gone through special glass also with anti-snooping devices built into it and also layered on top of it. Sadly for Mr Sum, it's not quite good enough to match our technology. At the moment, we're slightly ahead of him."

Georgi paused while Bond tried to take it all in.

"I can tell you," continued Georgi, "that Sum Taeyoung is not there today. Much of the time we know exactly where he is. Much of the time we can see him when we want to. But today he's got away from us. I'm not that bothered and if I was I could call in more help if I wanted to find him. Like satellite surveillance. But it's so expensive that unless I really need it I don't call on it."

The picture changed to a view of a city obviously taken from high altitude. Georgi again used the hand control and the picture zoomed closer and closer with first buildings then streets then crowds of people coming into view.

"If you couple that satellite imagery technology to camera identification technology then no longer is one person on the planet like - er - the needle in the haystack as you say. You can spot an individual you're trying to find however big the crowd he might be in. It just takes time."

The picture changed and Bond found himself looking at a picture of a very large man dressed in mid Eastern robes. But the man himself had an oriental look to him, had a mass of unwieldy hair that fell from his head to seemingly merge with an equally large mass of beard and bushy moustache. It was difficult to give him an age. Maybe mid 50s thought Bond. And as he watched, the picture - a studio type portrait - slowly changed to become an image of the same man but made up of thousands of bright green computer lines. And now, almost mesmerised by the screen, he saw the computerised image of the man turn 360 degrees before the view shot upwards to look down on his head and torso.

"He - or it - looks like a bush!" said Bond.

"George Bush?" quizzed Georgi with a hint of a laugh in his voice.

"No, don't be bloody daft. I mean an organic bush. All that hair!"

"Bond - let me introduce you to Sum Taeyoung, founder of SDBI and orchestrator of major catastrophic events. We know Mr Sum from every angle," said Georgi. "This digitised image means it's quite difficult for him to get away from our prying eyes. So when I need to know where he is, I guess about seven times out of 10 I can find him."

"We have all sorts of technology we can access - including this."

And the green graphic of Sum Taeyoung was replaced on the screen by a fast moving aerial view of a desert. Bond couldn't even guess where or what this was about. The aircraft was obviously flying at high speed and very, very low across a big flat area of sand with the occasional dried up river bed, clusters of huts and sand dunes. It was a pretty desolate place wherever it was.

"Welcome to Afghanistan," triumphed Georgi. "This is a live view. It's from an RAF Reaper drone being controlled from Nevada though recently the RAF can now control them from the UK. And so can we now - well, not directly from here but via the RAF's upgraded facilities at RAF Waddington in Lincolnshire. We've a direct connection to them and can actually direct the drones from here if we want to. It hasn't happened very often but we can if we have very good reason for doing so."

"So, with satellites, high performance, computer supported snooper cameras, ordinary street cameras, security cameras, drones and access to help from all the intelligence agencies of the West - and a few elsewhere - though we don't officially exist, we have a lot of power at our finger tips,"

The desert scene started to fade and Bond was about to ask Georgi a question when another image appeared on the screen, a black and white square with a pattern on it. Bond recognised it instantly as being a QR code.

"This," said Georgi still with a tinge of triumph in his voice. "Is the QR that was on the APTI letterhead that you found and gave to the Scottish police."

"How the hell did you get hold of that?" asked Bond in an increasing daze of bewilderment. "And when?"

Georgi nodded in the direction of the people in the room.

"We got hold of it a couple of days or so ago. Though we don't officially exist, we do have power. In fact, we have quite incredible power if and when we care to use it. So we pulled rank on the Scottish police and they duly sent it to us - with some reluctance I think. We've even opened it. Which is more than you or the Scottish police could do."

Throughout this session Nagriza had been looking at Bond, watching his reactions and being amused by his amazement as Georgi introduced the sequences on the screen. She had been leaning forward, elbows on the table, head cupped in her hands. Bond increasingly found her alluring and now and then snatched furtive glimpses at her. The way she was looking up at him, through her rich brown eyes, was sensuous and he felt like a caught out schoolboy when their eyes met. They were micro moments but Bond felt a growing closeness to Nagriza though he wondered if what he took to be returned interest was purely in his imagination - a phantasy or indeed simple wishful thinking. But now Nagriza sat up and it was she who took over the narrative from Georgi.

"Breaking into the QR wasn't much of a challenge to the team here," she said with undisguised pride. "The Scottish police had been" - she searched for the right English words - "frustrated in trying to break the code. It was complicated. Clever. But we did it."

She waved at the rest of the team.

"They are very good. Very clever."

Now the image on the screen changed again to a mass of text and diagrams. Bond found he was looking at a chess board with the moves from a game listed to its right.

"But," continued Nagriza with a smile and a half laugh "they're not that clever!" She emphasised the word "that" with a touch of sarcasm in the voice.

"We've broken into the QR and this is what we see. It seems like an account of a game of chess. As you can see, it's all in a foreign language - Russian. And it's a very sophisticated game of chess. Whoever was involved in playing this or designing it was a chess player of great skill. And possibly someone with a military background. There's a distinct battlefield strategy feel to it. What we've not been able to work out yet is what it means. We think the squares of the board represent places - and possibly time - and the pieces represent particular people, maybe. Not all the squares are involved and not all the pieces are involved. It's very complex and without the code it will be a challenge to break. And these pages and illustrations show a game that is played to an end. To you that's checkmate. In Russian, it's Shah Mat!"

Chapter 14

Sum Taeyoung knew exactly what the chess game was about. After all, he and his client had devised it. But of everyone involved, only Sum knew the whole extent of the plot, the most ambitious programme of global chaos he had ever conceived. Now the pieces on the chessboard were moving in the right direction, all heading to a particular date, a crescendo moment and the biggest achievement so far in Sum's dark career.

And, by the strangest of quirks and coincidences, had there have been a window in the room in which Bond now stood with Georgi and Nagriza in the basement communications centre of the European secret service, or had they indeed still been doing what an hour before they had been doing - gazing out of the window in Georgi's apartment toward the wide expanse of the River Thames, all three of them might have seen a boat speeding up the Thames between Greenwich and Westminster. And they would not have needed satellites or spy cameras or snoop aircraft. All they would have needed was keen eyesight because standing towards the bows of the boat, big, bold, conspicuous and upright like an Admiral inspecting his fleet, was the man Bond had so recently seen on a screen in the form of a three dimensional computer image. Long robed, long haired, Sum Taeyoung was in London.

There were two reasons for this. Typical of Sum, one was a legitimate business reason and the other had darker purposes. The second purpose totally focussed on a man he might have seen had that man still been looking out of the picture window at the passing boats and had Sum known where to look. Sum was in London to organise Bond's death!

The legitimate reason concerned an area in Jiangsu, the Yellow Sea coastal province in the north east of China. With a population of around 80 million, this part of China, like all others, was on a fast track modernisation programme which to Sum meant one thing. Opportunity! Appreciably more than most other parts of China, Jiangsu has openly courted skills from beyond its own boundaries and even the boundaries of China. There is more Western investment here than in most other Chinese provinces. This open policy meant that Sum had become aware of a need for particular help in an urban regeneration programme in the town of Wuxi. This dynamic town had established a reputation for not only its explosive economic growth but its development of solid connections with the world beyond China.

Like all other parts of Jiangsu, Wuxi suffered the consequences of monsoons. The town's progressive programme was being prejudiced by increasingly frequent incidents of severe flash flooding. Though they had been part of Jiangsu's climate since man had started to colonise this part of China, the effects of monsoons were becoming more difficult, disruptive and costly as urban areas grew in population with more roads, more buildings and more concreted areas spreading across the town. Thanks to his worldly experience and knowledge, when Sum saw their challenge he recalled a potential answer. The proven solution was in part of the Swedish town of Malmo where an English consultancy had once helped resolve a water and weather related problem as well as a social one.

The scheme there had been sparked when the local authority bowed to pressure from school children and agreed to build them somewhere they could deliver their plays and concerts. But, in an open competition, the winning design for the project was based on the three pillars of sustainable development. It provided economic, social and environmental benefits. The creative answer was an open air amphitheatre which not only provides the children with a stage for their performances but, when the weather is very wet and stormy, water that previously flooded the area in an uncontrolled manner is now caught in the amphitheatre which serves not only the needs of the children but acts as a storm water catchment system. Trapped water that would have otherwise flooded the area is released in a controlled way from the basin of the amphitheatre into open culverts that take the water to the nearby sea. The culverts themselves are open and designed to attract bird and plant life - biodiversity - which adds significantly to the aesthetic values of the area and in doing so raised property values.

Sum thought it a splendid project that provided an integrated, three dimensional solution. It was one he hoped to encourage the Jiangsu authorities to go for and for the English consultancy to deliver. Being the middleman, he hoped to profit from fees from both sides of the fence. It was a typical SDBI bread and butter project in the making. Sum had been to a meeting with the Greenwich based English consultants and now, on their behalf, he carried a proposition to be delivered to China. He had hired a launch to take him back along the Thames towards Westminster and to a pub where he was to meet a man who, hopefully, would serve his darker mission.

This mission, something which had been niggling at Sum for some time, had developed to be well beyond a mere irritant. Now it had to be dealt with. The trigger had been a message from Chan Yung.

"Someone has broken into my QR," said a trembling voice at the end of the phone. "I can tell that but I can't tell who or where. I just know it was and I know when. It was two days ago."

Sum was furious. And in his fury he undertook a value analysis of the bright young South Korean IT wizard. Clearly Chan was clever. Clearly he knew his way around the world of information technology as well as anyone on the planet. He was inventive and adventurous. But he was not unique. And also, clearly, he was clumsy and made mistakes.

On the other side of the Atlantic, as Sum headed for Westminster, another day was in its early breaking and New York was waking up. Chan and his young girlfriend had not been rushed to rise from bed. They rarely were. They often lay naked together in the warmth of the bed, just side by side, bodies just touching in comfort and reassurance to each other. They were still in bed this morning when the call bell to their apartment buzzed. They looked at each other in surprise. It was unheard of to have visitors at such an hour. Chan climbed from the bed and still without clothes on went to the intercom.

"Hello."

An unmistakable voice responded.

"Chan, it's me. Jo"

"Shit," responded Chan. "What do you want? And so early."

"Just let me in, you Korean Gook!"

Chan ducked the offence. "Give me two minutes."

He and the young girl hastily put some clothes on before Chan headed for the front door which he opened to let in a fairly disheveled Jo Summers.

"Hi," said Jo towards Chan's girlfriend while mentally cursing that he had forgotten Chan always had female company. It presented an added complication.

"What brings you here at this ungodly hour?" asked Chan.

"Sadly, this," replied Jo Summers whilst drawing a pistol from his jacket pocket and shooting Chan between the eyes. As Chan fell, the young Asian girl gave a half yelp which would have been a full scream had not a bullet from Jo Summers taken life away from her too.

Summers stood for a while looking at the result of his work. That was the quick and easy bit. The tidy up would take more time. He felt sad for Chan. He had got to know him and quite liked him. It was an early end to a talented young life but Summers had done what he had been told to do and that would earn him much face with Sum Taeyoung and a healthy bonus. Not that he had any option. An order from Sum was an order. There was no option. No alternative. What had to be done had to be done.

Back in London, with scant thought for the taking of life he had ordered in New York, Sum joined the growing London lunchtime hustle and left the river to head for the pub where he had arranged to meet another assassin. The news from Chan had crystalized one thing in Sum's mind. Bond had to go. It sounded like something out of a spy novel.

Chapter 15

Governor Al Williams had had many ambitions when he first won office but, on reflection, that had not included taking the State of California into independence. If anyone had voiced that as being one of his key objectives when he set out on his political career, he would have said it was a preposterous, ludicrous and even scurrilous idea. But now it seemed he had set a river running that he could not divert or dam even if he wanted to. The swell of support for the independence ticket had gained a momentum that was beyond anything he could ever have anticipated. In moments of honest reflection, it surprised, amazed and even scared him. But now it was unstoppable.

Direct communication with the President had all but dried up. There remained a hostile campaign by others in the White House and there was mixed reaction from the media. Some called him "Cavalier" or "Irresponsible" or even "Traitorous" while others labelled him "Visionary" and "Decisive". Across the State there were two distinct camps of opinion, those in favour and those not in favour and campaigners on both sides were energetic and noisy. Lobbying activity had become frenzied and dirty tricks were surfacing daily. But to a hardened professional politician, it was stuff that came with the job. But it did not take an expert to see that the groundswell of support for the Governor had continued to grow and by now most Californians fully anticipated independence. The only real remaining question was - when?

Negotiations with Jake Bloomer of APTI had continued against a backdrop of continuing flares of problems and challenges from UK legal representatives of Kemp and from the university. But news from APTI was consistently encouraging. The Chinese oil remained on offer and now dates for delivery were being mooted and practical facilities established by which to receive it. Across the State, and especially in the media, a debate raged about the comparison values, security, and even ethics of giving away to the Chinese an untried and unproven new Anglo/US technology that could potentially provide free energy - but with the word 'potential' massively underlined, versus shale gas with its controversial relationship with the environment and particularly the issue of how it potentially polluted groundwater and allegedly caused health problems, and free supply of oil from China. This deal raised its own set of questions - still largely unanswered. Why should China give away oil when it could not get enough to serve its constantly growing needs for more?

The media was having a field day debating the strengths and weaknesses of each proposition and campaign groups had developed around the alternative schemes. Experts seemed to be sprouting up all over the place and there were endless hours of debate on television.

The Governor had established an Independence Working Group to investigate all the consequences and the pros and cons of the split from the Union. This Group itself divided into topic areas - finance; legal and constitutional; energy; process. The energy sub group delved deeply into the options opened to the State and on a SWOT analysis concluded that the new fuel being developed by Kemp and the University was exciting but could have a very long gestation period between research and production and delivery.

Fracking, the process of extracting shale gas, was creating a transformation of the energy industry despite environmental issues hanging over it which, in a few parts of the US, was slowing progress as planning constraints responded to the environmental doubts.

And then there was the remarkable offer of free oil in a contra deal for the new, unproven technology from Kemp and the University. However much they talked, debated and tested the three options, it was the Chinese proposition which consistently prevailed. After yet another specialist 'Think Tank', an exhausting debate into the early hours of the evening, event Chairman, Senator Charlie Mullring said, with something of great impatience in his voice; "We're going round and round in circles - wasting time and money - and getting very frustrated and heated about this. To me it's now simple. However much we run this thing, however many times we take it round and round more and more debates, we come to the same conclusion. It's a no brainer! The Chinese deal wins every time."

Meanwhile, the group delegated with issues of process strengthened discussions with the United Nations and a plan for a global Declaration of Independence was in the course of being drafted by State experts and lawyers with help from the UN. After many frustrating efforts to engage with the UN, a close working relationship had eventually been established with DESA, the United Nations Department of Economic and Social Affairs. This organisation and others from which it had been derived, had a long and successful history of helping countries around the world meet their economic, social and environmental challenges. Indeed, its stated mission says *'it promotes development for all - reflects a fundamental concern for equity and equality in countries large and small, developed and developing'*.

To Governor Williams that seemed to fit the bill admirably though he thought it unlikely that those who wrote it would ever have expected it to be helping California leave the United States of America to become an independent Nation and the ninth biggest economy on the planet! The same thoughts had been in the mind of Sum Taeyoung some time ago when he first made moves that were now resulting in DESA becoming associated with another square in his chess game.

The Governor was musing on these matters late in the evening, shoes off and feet on his desk, legs outstretched and his back leaning deeply into his reclined chair, a glass of chilled beer in his left hand, when the phone rang. Cursing this interruption to a sublime moment of solitude and reflection, Governor Williams sat up and reached for his phone.

"Yes," he said. The voice at the other end was his private secretary.

"Governor, I have had a message - or more like an invitation - from DESA."

She paused. He encouraged her to continue.

"They're offering you a time and a place for the Declaration," she said, again pausing afterwards. With no response from the Governor, she continued.

"Apparently they have their Annual Symposium, this year in Montreux in Switzerland - on Lake Geneva - and they're inviting you to be the key guest speaker and to use that opportunity to announce the Declaration."

"Wow," responded the Governor, taken by surprise at this progressive turn of events. The UN in all its guises, including DESA, was a slow and cumbersome beast out of which moments of decisiveness seem to appear only rarely. So the Governor was taken a bit off guard.

"That's out of the blue. Have they got a date?"

"Yes Sir," his assistant said with a growing sense of impending explosions. "It's in 10 days time!"

Chapter 16

The journey north by train from London was tedious. Bond regretted that the Porsche was stuck in the car park in Inverness airport. However, it was made easier by the presence of Nagriza who had insisted she accompany Bond when Georgi had made his suggestion.

"Look, Bond," he had said. "While we fight the same enemy - fight the same battle - we should be together. You should move in with us in London while this is going on."

And Bond had agreed but told Georgi he would first have to go to his house in the Midlands to ensure that it was still alright and to pick up some things. Georgi had understood that. He didn't object. He was even supportive when Nagriza said she would go with him. So they had travelled by train to Birmingham and by taxi south out of the city.

Bond's house stood on what had once been a main artery road leading south out of Birmingham. It was significantly quieter now since a nearby bypass had opened. Standing back from the road and behind some significant hedges, the four-square mock Tudor looking building was, as Bond told people, "only" a four bedroomed city house. But it did have a lot of character, did stand alone, and it did have adjacent fields leading out to the Warwickshire countryside. This was the fringes of the urban giant with just a few nearby shops and a pub with a busy restaurant.

It was sheer co-incidence that Bond had bought both this house, and the crofter's cottage in Scotland, at knock down prices when both were in serious need of love and attention. For those who did not know otherwise, Bond looked like a property speculator, buying dilapidated properties cheaply, modernising and improving them, then selling them off. The fact that he had sold neither showed that the truth was he had bought what he had liked and what he could afford and at a pace his work and finances would allow. He had improved both over a period of time, doing bits of simple work himself but bringing in friendly professionals to do most of the complicated stuff. The Birmingham property gave him a base that was centrally located in England which was useful as his work could take him anywhere, was close to the motorway network and to Birmingham airport.

Bond and Nagriza had agreed with Georgi to return to London the following day. Bond, the word of the Scottish policeman echoing in his mind from the call he had received outside the House of Commons, was relieved to find the house intact and no signs of any intrusion, unlike the cottage in Scotland. Nagriza was like a child with a new toy and excitedly explored the house from top to bottom. Bond introduced her to the room she would use overnight.

In the lounge Bond lit a coal fire and supplemented the coal with logs he carried in from the substantial log pile at the rear of the house. The evening was dry but distinctly chilly and threatening rain. But, despite that, Nagriza eagerly agreed to Bond's suggestion that they go for a short walk around the area surrounding the house then to the pub for an evening meal.

Heading from the back of the house away from the main road, Nagriza found Bond leading her through a grassy meadow to a small wood of mainly silver birch. After days in London and the claustrophobic train journey the freshness of the evening air, the smell of the open countryside and the walk were exhilarating. They had been walking for some 15 minutes before Bond realised Nagriza was holding his hand. For him it was a moment of tingling significance. He had no idea what it meant to her. But he was thrilled and it started his imaginative thoughts again about this girl who he found so alluring.

The pub was pretty quiet, it being mid-week. They took a table for two in a darkened corner of the restaurant area. Their nearest fellow diners were some way away. It gave Bond an opportunity to unravel the mystery of this stunning woman who now sat with him.

"What brought you to the UK?" he asked as an opening shot.

Nagriza was leaning forward from her chair, elbows on the table, head cupped in her hands so that she had to look up at Bond as she replied. This had happened to him at Georgi's apartment, those brown eyes, looking upwards towards him. It was like a man-trap! He began to wonder if she did it on purpose but then that was to be presumptuous. Why should she flirt with him? She obviously lived with Georgi.

"It is a story of coincidences," she replied. "When I was younger I lived with my parents in the south of Uzbekistan. My father had been a fisherman but his life had been ruined by what happened to the sea in which he used to fish."

"Where was that?" asked Bond though with a growing sense of anticipation, he thought he knew the answer already.

"The Aral Sea," she replied.

"Good God!" responded Bond, amazed at the coincidence that had brought them together. Now he really did start to wonder if fate was playing a game between the two of them. He delayed responding while a waiter took their orders.

"The story of the Aral Sea," he told her, "is one of the things that motivated me to become involved with sustainable development. And now I find it's your homeland. That's incredible!"

"Why were you interested in the Aral Sea?" she asked.

"From school boy days." he responded. "I've had a long-time fascination with maps and things like ancient trading routes. In England it was the salt routes. But as I become more adventurous I found the story of the Ottoman Empire - and the Silk Route - Marco Polo and Alexander the Great - Genghis Khan - things like that. As a youngster I found it all very romantic - the stuff of schoolboy adventures and colourful heroes. I found it wondrous that so long ago people were trading from as far afield as China to the Mediterranean and onward to the European coast of the

North Atlantic Ocean. The Ottoman Empire was enormous and incredibly influential and seems somehow to have been lost to history."

He stopped, concerned he was boring her. But she was obviously intent on what he was saying.

"Some years later, not that long ago really, I was reading some stuff about the Empire which just happened to be about Uzbekistan. That led me to the story of the Aral Sea. I was horrified by what I read. I don't need to tell you that what had been the world's fourth largest inland sea was now reduced down to a filthy, chemical sludge-like puddle. I saw pictures of it. I couldn't believe it. I could see what I then thought looked like quaint Cornish-like seaside villages and little ports but with small fishing boats keeled over to one side on dry land. The water's edge was now 30 miles and more away."

"One of those boats might have been my father's," mused Nagriza.

Bond shook his head. The coincidences were extraordinary. He continued: "I started to look for more to read about it and the more I read the more shocking I found it. It was inconceivable to me that this was a manmade disaster. But it was. You know it was. Soviet engineers had diverted the sea's feeder rivers to irrigate the cotton fields and so no new water topped up the sea as it evaporated - like all inland seas do. So the water in the sea got less and less, the ratio of slime and gunge to water got bigger and bigger, and enormous health problems started to spread across the area. Right?"

"Right!" Nagriza was delighted and impressed he knew so much but equally depressed by the memories he was stirring.

"And," continued Bond "I thought to myself - what the hell are we doing to ourselves? What are we doing to our planet? It seemed an example of sheer madness gone even crazier - another example of money dictating everything and causing people to make incredibly stupid decisions. It is stupid when you think about it. The economic benefits to the cotton industry must have been outweighed by the enormous economic costs to the fishing fleet - so to food provision - and to the cost of helping people with health problems caused by what was going on. But then I found more and more examples around the world. The Aral Sea story was a defining moment in my life and switched me on to the subject of sustainable development."

"And that's where I lived," said Nagriza triumphant in the coincidence. Quietly and with a voice increasingly full of emotion, she told Bond: "Originally we lived almost at the water's edge. But slowly the sea declined and the water slipped further and further away. It was terrible. Yes - there was a lot of illness in the area and no work. Families scratched a living. I was incredibly lucky. There were scientific teams around researching the Aral Sea story and its health consequences to the local population. I was very curious and interested in what they were doing and sort of edged my way into one of the teams. Because I had nothing else to do I used to carry stuff for them, run messages - anything to feel an involvement - anything that gave some sort of meaning to day by day life. It gave me some sort of - er - reason for life which I hadn't had until then. I was 16 at the time."

She gathered her thoughts and Bond could easily see the telling of this story was paining her. But she continued: "That lasted nearly a year. The team I was with was a UN funded team. It came from Belgium. When they finished their work, I was so much part of the team they asked me if I would like to go to Belgium with them and they offered me a proper job - a menial assistant job - and some training. It was a fantastic opportunity. I jumped at it."

"But to enable me to do that I needed official Uzbekistan papers. That's not easy in Uzbekistan. Nothing is easy in Uzbekistan!" She paused. "It is very bureaucratic and corrupt. Getting the documentation proved almost impossible. I spent days in Tashkent, often sleeping rough and with hardly any food. But I got to know one or two civil servants and one of them took a liking to me. He was a bit of a bully and very arrogant but I found he worked for the SNB. It took me some time to find out that was the Uzbekistan National Secret Service but by then I was - er - a very close friend to this man and he eventually got me a secretary job with the SNB."

"Once in, I worked hard and I find out a lot. I find things out about some of my superiors and I get a better job. Then I start working on projects for them and one was about SDBI. That took me to meeting Georgi. The rest is - how do you say - history!"

There was a pause before Bond said anything: "And now you work for the European Secret Service - that doesn't exist!"

"Yes," she replied with a shy smile and almost a whisper.

There was a silence between them for a moment.

"And you're Georgi's lady?"

"No!"

"But you live together."

"Yes."

"And you sleep together."

"Sometimes."

There was another silence before she added: "It's a convenience. I am very fond of Georgi. And he got me the job. That is very good of him. And he is a very nice man. We are very good friends. And it is a very pressurised job. Sometimes it's exciting. Sometimes it's dangerous. Sometimes it's very routine and boring. So we help each other. We look after each other. We are fond of each other - no more. And sometimes we have sex. It helps the tension. It helps cope. It is convenient."

Bond felt a strain suddenly between the two of them, but by the time a waiter had delivered their food it was over, a passing moment of doubts and discomfort. They ate and talked.

"Do you miss home?" Bond asked.

"Of course I do," Nagriza responded. "Everyone misses home when they are not where home is. And I feel guilty that I am now in a different life - a different world - with the comforts of life, good health and good food. It is easy to take it for granted. But I remember when I had none of these things. And I try and help my family even if I don't see them very often."

"It is a difficult world for many people," Bond reflected.

"Yes. I find it hard to believe that when people live in places like London, New York, Paris, even Moscow - they have such comfort, but huge amounts of people elsewhere in the world have no regular food, no water, no roof over their heads - no future. Only despair."

"I remember," recalled Bond "years ago reading about the expectation of a Great Walk North - the destitute people of Africa rising and heading North for Europe and the promise of everything they had not got. In a way you can see that happening around the world, people trying to get into Gibraltar, into Australia, across the border from Mexico into the US - people trying to get into the UK."

"Gene - it's just disgusting that in the 21st century so many people have so much and so many people have so little." Bond could hear the emotion in Nagriza's voice. He had a growing admiration for her compassion which seemed to fit uncomfortably with her career as a counter espionage spy. What an enigma she was.

"It's an invitation to those who want to cause trouble," she continued. "And so often the politicians either don't see it - don't understand it - or are so corrupted they don't do anything about it."

"Corruption's one of the world's great evils," said Bond.

"But lack of hope is tragic." Again, Nagriza was having trouble spilling the words out, so powerful were the emotions within her. "People must have hope Gene. You know, I thought the word 'Kamikaze' was something buried in the history of World War Two. I thought people who were willing to commit suicide so as to cause damage to other people was something that belonged in the past. But now - well - it's almost commonplace. That's more than tragic. That life has become so cheap - so expendable. But I see so much around the world where people have nothing but despair - where there is not just a gap between those who have and those who haven't but between the people and the politicians too. How can that be? Politicians become politicians because people vote for them. So how is it that politicians so often don't seem to be looking after their people? I do not understand it. Look at places like Greece and Portugal. People marching because they fear for their futures."

"Yes," he agreed. "And how extraordinary people marched in Brazil because of the money being spent on a football tournament. They saw it as an injustice against the people in Brazil who have nothing. Fancy that happening in Brazil! In Brazil of all places. A football crazy country. It seems to me nothing is impossible at the moment."

"Gene - I think the world is in a terrible mess. I worry for the future."

"So do I," agreed Bond grimly.

And in sombre mood they left, Bond paying the dinner bill before they headed outside to find it was raining heavily. They ran the distance back to Bond's house where they arrived soaked. It kind of broke the gloom that had got into their minds and, like children, they had the giggles as they stood inside the house dripping.

"I think I will take a shower," she announced.

"Me too. You first." he said.

"No," she said firmly. "We shower together".

She paused.

"It will be environmentally friendly. We will save water."

And they laughed again, water still dripping from them.

Chapter 17

There are so many imponderables to take into account when trying to kill someone at a distance. Only a highly proficient marksman can make any guarantees of success, and even then the unexpected can unexpectedly come into play. What looks to be a clean shot can, in an instant, be corrupted by outside influences.

Sum's hired assassin had researched Bond at length, well, best he could in the limited time available. He researched all his targets and he would have liked to have had more time to research Bond. But there was precious little time given before the client's deadline and now there was no time to lose. The client wanted a quick job. It was not too difficult. Bond ran a very open life. So the hired assassin knew that Bond had two properties, one in Scotland and one near Birmingham. He knew the addresses of both. So though there had been little time between being given the assignment and Bond heading north, it did not take much of a guess that when Bond booked tickets for Birmingham, he was heading home.

So the assassin headed for Birmingham too - in fact on the same train as Bond and Nagriza. That Bond was accompanied was of little concern. The girl was very attractive and obviously a very close friend. He had not had time to research her. He had no idea who she was except she was obviously and very openly a close companion to Bond. And though this professional assassin had a niggling concern that he had not done his homework on the girl as he would have liked to, the client wanted a fast kill - and had paid a good sum in advance with the 50% balance payable on result. This rare demonstration of professional negligence was to prove costly.

As he knew where Bond lived, there was no thought of following the two of them when he watched them leave the station at Birmingham in a taxi. To have followed them would have been risky and unnecessary. So the assassin arrived on the edge of Birmingham and near to Bond's house when Bond and Nagriza happened to be in the pub. It gave him time enough for a quick and close look around. He noted the general geography of the house and painted a picture of it in his mind - the location of the doors to the house, the shape and extent of the front drive, the high hedge across the front of the property but the wide gap between the gate posts but absence of a gate. The front lawn extended right to the front door but ended on the right where the shale drive stretched from the gates to the garage adjacent the house. During this reconnaissance process he came to the conclusion the house was empty and that Bond and the girl had gone off somewhere, presumably, he guessed right, to eat out.

Opposite Bond's house was an extensive open area, mostly unused but with some buildings that seemed to form some sort of dilapidated builders' yard. It was surrounded by wire fencing but seemed to have little or no security. Certainly there were no guard dogs and no cameras. Also, helpfully, the street lighting was poor with many areas of near darkness around the perimeter fence. He was thankful for that as he cut an entrance and crept through the fencing, tugging his large holdall through after him. As he did so it started to rain. He turned his collar up on his dark coloured jacket.

His luck was very much with him. A single storey building, decaying and with broken windows, stood not quite opposite the entrance to Bond's house. In the semi dark of the dying day, he scrambled round the back and used a drainpipe to climb to the roof. The assassin truly thanked his lucky stars because the building was so located that, from the roof, there was a clear view of Bond's front door. It was an uncluttered line of sight. A clean shot from where he lay on the roof, passing the end of the hedge on the left and diagonally across the front corner of the lawn to the front door. It was a great piece of good fortune.

During the next hour, keeping his profile low on the roof but with darkness now arriving to help his concealment, he extracted the sections of the rifle - an American Cheytac .408 calibre - with its long barrel, tripod, and intricate sight mechanism. It was an almost automatic procedure and like working with an old friend. They had operated together for quite some years. With the weapon complete, he took time to work out the distance from here to the selected point of hit.

He created a cradle on which to rest the front end of the rifle's barrel. With it now raining hard and night firmly arrived, he cowered under the lightweight but waterproof and camouflaged sheet that he had pulled from the bag. Passing traffic had been few and far between and nobody had actually walked past the builder's yard while he had been there. The only people he saw, caught fleetingly in the street lights, were Bond and Nagriza running back to the house, obviously anxious to escape the rain.

He waited another hour before convincing himself nothing was going to happen until morning. Clambering back down to ground level, he found himself a way into the building and settled down to get a few hours sleep. He would be awake before daybreak, alert and rehearsed for the job to do. All he had to do now was wait.

Across the road, Bond had agreed to Nagriza's command and they had laughed and joked as they showered together. It was in the aftermath that she had stood before him, her breasts deliberately and teasingly only just touching his chest, her hands cupping his chin to bring him to her for a gentle, exploratory, lingering kiss while their naked bodies responded to their closeness. In bed, Nagriza had proved to be a talented and skilful lover. Bond found her touch exquisite, gentle at times, gripping at others, passive and aggressive in contrasting moments. When he was able to see her eyes - when she was mounted on top of him, their rich brownness seemed to challenge him, to take them to greater heights of adventure. He, in turn, took her several times to the brink of explosion, stopping short of doing so, leaving her high on crests of ecstasy and agony, her finger nails digging into him as she reacted and responded to what he was doing to her. It had quickly become apparent that they both excelled and delighted in giving pleasure as much as they did in receiving it and that the sexual drive to be as if one body was shared between them. She, in turn, coaxed and teased him, nibbling down his body, her breasts rubbing against his chest, his waist and then his groin as she progressed down his body to a point where he found control almost impossible.

Their passionate encounter lasted deep into the night, passing many crescendo peaks and ranging from quiet and tender moments to others that were vigorous, physical and noisy. In the end, exhausted and spent, they lay side by side, still intoxicated by their naked togetherness, and drifted into sleep.

When dawn arrived Bond was the first to wake. He lay for a while looking at the girl to his side, the whiteness of her body, the hazel hair. Eventually he made a move to get out of bed, but his stirring was enough to rouse her. She looked at him and smiled, and caught hold of him and enticed and guided him towards her.

"No," he said. "We must get up and get moving."

"No," she said. And she won - again - as he succumbed to her sensuality.

It was an hour later that he finally escaped.

Across the road, the night had been far less comfortable and adventurous. It had been damp and smelly, but the assassin had dozed and even slept. His military training and experience had helped. He was awake before daylight and had crept over the road and around the house, departing with the reassurance that Bond and the girl were still inside.

Again he checked distances, the strength of the gusting cross wind, his getaway route - all routine matters that he did more or less automatically. Eventually he settled down to wait.

It was quite some time before he saw a car - a private hire taxi - drive between the gate posts to park on the drive. Lying with legs spread, the rifle held steady on its tripod and his make do cradle, sights locked onto the front door, safety catch off, he waited, controlling his breathing, keeping all his nerves and his heart beat steady and well in control. He saw the door open and the girl step out with Bond right behind her. She interrupted his line of fire. But he waited - holding the shot - holding his fire - seeing the hairline sights first on her, then, increasingly as he came more fully into sight, on Bond. The plan had always been a head shot and now the assassin had a full, clear view of his target. His squeeze on the trigger was as it always was - as he had been trained for it to be - gentle, hardly a breath of pressure. He felt the recoil as the bullet left.

But - there are so many imponderables to take into account when trying to kill someone at a distance.

Bond, following Nagriza from the house, was loaded with an overnight case, a computer case, various odds and ends he wanted to take to London, and other bits and pieces. He should have made two trips to the taxi but instead he had loaded himself up. Which is why his grip on his house keys was poor. Which is why he dropped them. Which is why he bent to pick them up - which created one of those imponderables that even the most hardened, practiced and professional assassins cannot plan for.

Bond heard a loud thud above him and felt splinters of wood and bits of brick hit his head. The bullet meant for him had bedded itself in the door frame, shattering an upright section.

"What the fuck was that?" exclaimed Bond, clearly not understanding what had happened but reacting to the sound and the bits of wood that now hit him.

"Get behind the car!" yelled Nagriza and Bond did not hesitate. He heard clearly and unmistakably the sound of the second shot, then another. Bullets this time hit the brickwork of the house just above where he was crouching behind the back of the taxi. Shattered bits of brick and brick dust flew in all directions, some hitting Bond. With the second shot he understood what was going on. After the third he waited to see if more were going to be fired.

"Christ!" he thought. "Under fire again!"

"What the hell's going on mate?" The voice behind him was a gruff, male one with a strong Birmingham accent. Bond turned to see it was the taxi driver, now cowering behind him.

"Someone's taking pot shots at us," said Bond. "I suggest you make a run for the house. Safest place I reckon. The door's still open. I was trying to shut it when the first shot went off."

And with no further comment the driver was off, sprinting for the front door of the house which was only twenty feet away and reaching it with no more shots fired.

Bond peered round from the back of the taxi and risked a look in the direction he thought the shots had come from. To his horror he was just in time to catch sight of Nagriza running, crouched low and zig zagging towards the road, hand gun held steady and ready for action in her right hand. His heart sank. It pounded within him. He waited a full minute before moving, his overwhelming worry about Nagriza outweighing concerns for his own safety though his progress to the gate was cautious. He had only just got there when, from over the road, somewhere in the builders' yard, two shots rang out. He sprinted across the road, waiting for a third shot, waiting for the thud of a bullet hitting him, ending it all. Another shot rang out, somewhere in the yard, somewhere over to the left and certainly not aimed at him.

Concern for his own wellbeing diminishing and worry about Nagriza growing, he moved along the security fence not knowing what to do but needing to do something. He realised it was raining. In fact he was soaked but it was not something to concern him. He came to a gap in the fence, somewhere where someone had obviously cut their way into the yard. The wire fence was open, low down to the ground and with ragged ends to the wire mesh pushed back. He crawled through and, once inside, stayed low and still trying to work out where the shots had come from, listening for any movement. But the morning was silent except for the sound of falling rain and traffic in the distance.

In front of him a dilapidated building stood with dirty, cobweb strewn broken windows of jagged glass and a door ajar. He risked a sprint to it, diving into the building and thankful for the lack of gunfire. The building was empty, the floor littered with rubble - and some sort of sleeping bag - or at least a cover that was in camouflage greens and browns. It looked out of place and obviously was. It clearly belonged to whoever had fired the shots at him - who Nagriza was now up against. He crossed gently over to a window, trying desperately to be as quiet as possible which was difficult as the floor was littered with brick debris, broken glass and general rubbish. But he made it safely to the opposite side and looked out of the window.

There was open space between this building and another, equally run down but without a door or any windows that he could see. There was plenty of rubble and discarded machinery between the two buildings and growing puddles glistening in the morning light and rippling in the now intense rain.

It was a full couple of minutes before more shots rang out and he saw the unmistakable figure of Nagriza run from the other side of the nearby building, gun still in hand, soaked hazel hair flying as she scampered around an end of the wall and out of his sight again. More shots rang out. To his right.

Was it instinct or something else? Bond crept out of the building he had been sheltering in and ran to his right, circumnavigating the broken down building in front of him. He ran, bent forward as he had seen Nagriza run, splashing through puddles, rain getting into his eyes. He reached the seemingly comparative safety of the nearest wall and picked up enough courage to peer round the corner. Nobody was there but there was a doorway, this one without a door. He moved forward slowly and warily towards it, peering in. Again, nobody. But from somewhere nearby he heard a foot scrape against something. Was it Nagriza or was it the gunman? He thought the sound had come from outside the building he was now entering. To his right Bond saw a stone staircase littered with debris, dust and bits and pieces. He made his way gingerly to it, his heart beat pounding in his ears like a set of drums, trying to control his breathing which sounded so loud to him that anyone nearby would also hear it. He picked his way slowly through the mess on the floor, petrified about not generating any sound to betray his presence. He was relieved to reach the upper floor without making much of a noise. There was a window. It was in the other end wall, around the corner from the ground floor door through which he had entered the building. Slowly, cautiously, he crept forward and equally warily peered out and down from the window.

There below him stood a figure. A man. Wearing a dark jacket that was shining in its wetness. Slung over his shoulder was a long barrelled rifle with some sort of complex sighting gear attached. He was holding a hand gun. He was rock still, seemingly, waiting.

Bond looked round. The floor was littered with bits and pieces. Amongst the clutter and dust Bond spied a workman's vice, probably heavy enough to cause damage, light enough for Bond to lift - just. He moved carefully towards it, gently heaved it up and carried it to the window. The figure below still remained, motionless, gun poised. Bond knew he had one chance and if his move did not work the consequences could be catastrophic. It took all the strength he could muster to lift the heavy vice, move it into the window frame, then lift it further so as to heave it in the right direction. Looking very cautiously out from the window he could still see the dark coated figure below. As Bond looked down, so the figure below glanced up, caught sight of Bond and swung the hand gun round. Bond gave one last heave and the vice left his grip. He watched it fall and saw the gunman move to avoid it. For an instance Bond thought he was going to succeed. But, in his haste to move, the gunman stumbled on some debris. It slowed him enough for Bond's bomb to hit his target. The gunman fell to the floor in a crumpled heap.

Bond ran down the stairs and out into the rain.

"Nagriza!" he shouted. "Nagriza - it's all OK."

He looked down at the fallen gunman. There was a lot of blood. It seemed to be coming from his head. Bond wondered if he was dead. As a precaution, he kicked the hand gun away.

Still Nagriza had not appeared. Bond went to look for her. It did not take long to find her, still crouched down, hiding behind a corner of the building by the fence. As he approached she stood.

"I think I may have killed him," Bond said.

"That's good," she responded. "That's very good."

Her voice was faint, almost a whisper. And it quivered with emotion, strain, fatigue, fear.

"Hold me Gene. Hold me tight," she whispered.

He put his arms round her and felt her body melt into his. She was trembling. He stroked her soaked hair. In the distance he could hear the faint sound of sirens. He became aware of something liquid and sticky in his left hand. He took it from her and looked. It was covered in blood. Nagriza's blood.

Chapter 18

Deep down in the cellar-based communications centre of the European Secret Service, Georgi and the rest of the team - Jamie, Alan and Jane - had been devoting their time to trying to break the code on the QR printed on the APTI letterhead. Opening it had not been that much of a challenge to the team, contrasting to the failure of the Scottish police. The entry had been surrounded by codes and sub codes, some with destructive trigger devices that would obliterate the content if pursued wrongly. So the team wasn't surprised it had thwarted others.

The chess game revealed was a real puzzle. It showed a very aggressive black attack that from the outset swept all before it as the Black Queen drove down the board, capturing white pieces left and right and finally arriving at the far end of the board to corner the White King in a checkmate. It was a very spirited series of moves that made the game exceptionally one-sided and with a strategy centred on the fast movement of the Queen. To the side of the board there appeared to be what they took as a running commentary noting the moves, with a string of letters against each move. They were in Russian. There was extensive text against some moves and less in others. When translated, it was immediately obvious that some sort of code was being used. They were left with just a jumble of meaningless letters. The only bit that was clear and totally understandable was the final, uncoded words which were an emphatic and triumphant 'Shah Mat.'

The four of them were convinced the game concealed something else. Why otherwise was it within this heavily guarded QR?

"Why use a chess game to convey a coded message?" asked Georgi. "Why a chess game? Why not an ordinary encrypted message?"

"Russians like their chess," responded Jane.

"That's as may be. But why a chess game to convey a message?" repeated Georgi.

"Is it some famous Russian chess move?" Jamie poised the question almost rhetorically.

That seemed worthy of exploration and they spent a long time searching the Web for reports of past, famous Russian chess victories. There were many and each they looked at took time to consider. But they could find none that looked anything like the game they had before them with the domination of the Black Queen.

"We've got this wrong," said Alan eventually. "The games we've been looking at involve Russian Chess Masters. Chess Masters mostly play other Chess Masters unless they're doing some sort of public display. And no Chess Master would play such a crass bad game as whoever was the White player in our game."

The others agreed. It had been worth exploring but a complete red herring. They went back to the beginning.

"So if it's not a coded message," mused Georgi. "What else could it be?"

"Some sort of instructions, maybe," suggested Jane.

"Or orders," added Alan.

They struggled through a list of suggestions, none inspiring any confidence that they were on the right track.

"How about going back to the basic principles of codes," said Jane. "Do the board squares translate into anything? Or maybe the squares on which the Black Queen progresses means something."

So they tried that. In terms of places on the board where the Black Queen actually stopped, there were 10 squares. They noted each square's position in Russian then tried a variety of well used techniques to discover any hidden messages. With key words - 'Russia' and 'chess' - forming the basis of their research, their activity sent them down a variety of routes including variable length codes and different forms of cyphers and even into the strange worlds of Rosicrucians, with their variations in the game, and the Knights Templar. It produced nothing.

The group fell into a further period of gloomy silence. After a while, Georgi said: "The Black Queen progresses across the board in a series of steps. Right?"

They agreed.

"So it's like a journey - or a pathway. Right?"

There were nods of agreement.

"So what we're looking at isn't a message, it's a pathway - or the moves in a plan. Each move the Queen takes might be a progression towards an end objective and the jumble of letters against each square might be what has to - or has - happened at that step."

"You might be right," said Alan. "In which case it would be mighty useful to know what and where the Black Queen is when she gets to the point of checkmate."

Georgi agreed. "Of course it would. In fact, it would be fantastic if we could find what each move of the Queen means, if they mean anything. Can we go back to one square that the Queen has touched and see if we can find what it means. If we can break one, we can probably break them all."

They agreed. They also agreed they might as well go for broke and focus on the last square, the checkmate or shah mat square.

Jamie took responsibility for driving the computers as others fed him ideas.

It was a slow process and it was late into the day - about the same time Bond had taken Nagriza to dinner - when they decided enough was enough and they would return to it fresh in the morning.

Because of the dedication and commitment of those involved none of them switched off from the challenge overnight. With no computer help at their respective homes because of security reasons, all four of them reverted to paper scribbling.

It was Jane who offered the biggest new idea from the individual brain storming that had gone on through the night. When they reassembled at eight in the morning, each in turn offered any thoughts they had had during the night. Jane, who had been noticeably and uncharacteristically quiet since she arrived, mused about her idea in her mind and was the last to speak.

"Why are we focusing on Russian all the time?" she asked.

"Because it's written in Russian," responded Georgi, almost dismissively but wondering what line of thought this was.

"But didn't you tell us that APTI was a discreet subsidiary of SDBI?"

"I did," agreed Georgi.

"But SDBI is South Korean based, not Russian," said Jane. "What happens if we translate the text on the game from Russian to South Korean? Does that help?"

"It's worth a shot," responded Georgi and they got to it, Jamie making the changes on the computer then starting to see if the text or the square references made any new sense now.

Georgi's phone rang out and he broke away from the others to answer it. They were so engrossed they were oblivious to what Georgi was saying and his change of expression and body language. It was only when he returned to them they saw the colour had drained from him and his shoulders were now slumped as if bearing the weight of all the world's problems. He told them what the interrupting call had been about.

"It was Gene," said Georgi. "Gene Bond. Phoning from Birmingham. Nagriza's been shot. Gene doesn't know how badly. Seems someone took a pot shot at him and Nagriza got into some sort of gun fight and has been hit. I don't know how badly but it doesn't sound good. I need to go there as fast as I can. Jamie - you'll come with me. While we do that, can someone throw a security screen around the site of the shooting in Birmingham? I don't want the police all over this. We need to do that quickly before the police get too entrenched in it. I'll leave Gene's mobile number with you. He'll tell you where it happened and you can relay that to me. Bond thinks he's killed the man who shot Nagriza. It's a real mess. I need to see if we know the gunman. Bond's taking Nagriza to the Queen Elizabeth Hospital in Birmingham. There's a big military section there. I've told him to book her in via that. We can control things better that way. While one of you sorts the security net, can another sort the hospital and both of you keep going with the chess game? I'm gone - but keep me up to speed with all developments."

And with that Georgi and Jamie left.

Chapter 19

The Music and Convention Centre in Montreux has become internationally respected and renowned for being home to the town's annual jazz festival. It stands on the shores of the superbly picturesque Lake Geneva, separated from the waters' edge by borders of flowers and a pathway that is a popular walkway for sauntering elderly couples, young lovers wrapped in their own worlds and oblivious to the stunning surroundings, individual business people seeking escape from the tedium of the numerous corporate events now staged in the labyrinth of rooms in the Centre, and energetic roller blade skaters. Either side of the hardly graceful, very square profile of the Centre, but distanced by significant open spaces also given to colourful flower beds and areas of regularly manicured grass, are some of the many hotels of the town that cater for visiting tourists and visitors to the Centre. Across the lake, the spectacular Dents-du-Mido mountains tower into the skies with more snow-capped Alpine mountains to left and right. It is an idyllic setting for worldly events, musical concerts and business and political conferences.

Preparations advanced at the Music and Convention Centre ahead of the DESA Summit, the annual meeting of the United Nations Department for Economic and Social Affairs. Some 600 delegates from around the world would soon assemble for this three day event. Usually it would pass with minimal notice. It no doubt excited those involved, but to the world outside those directly involved with DESA, there was little interest. This was not the case now. This year's conference had attracted the world's media in huge numbers, all of them excited in anticipation of the much awaited declaration of independence by the US State of California. This was now top of the bill and strategically placed in the programme to be the crescendo moment of the Summit on day three.

The practical ramifications of this escalation of interest meant appreciably more security than usual at DESA's annual event. Now there seemed to be a developing state of chaos as the local police, national Swiss Militia and US special officers all tried, but were not always succeeding, in cooperating to establish a blanket security screen in and around the concrete, square profiled Music and Convention Centre. This included the lakeside pathway and its decorative flower beds - and even where from his small wooden hut a burly, youthful, shaved headed man usually hires his rowing boats and pedalos to tourists keen to enjoy the delights of the lake. All were sealed off by a police barrier, patrolled even during the event build up by a generous allocation of officers from the assembled international corps of law enforcers.

In London, Sum Taeyoung watched his chess game developing and started to put in place detail around the concluding moves. He now knew the date and the location for the Shah Mat were secure. He just needed to finesse the coup de grace. As part of this final act, Jo Summers and Jake Bloomer were now heading for Switzerland. They believed they knew the full plot, but they did not. Even at this late stage, Sum alone knew the full plan in which Jo Summer, Jake Bloomer and Asian Pacific Trading Inc were all now on borrowed time. This is why the effectiveness of Sum's Chinese walls between APTI and SDBI were paramount. He was happy to discard the distanced subsidiary company and two of its key men. But the consequences of what he plotted would be well distanced from both him and SDBI which he needed to live on, to scheme more plots and more globally de-stabling chaos.

In the glittering Siberian city of Kranoyarsk, Viktor Blucher sat in his office contemplating the latest news from Sum Taeyoung. In the coded conversation of their recent telephone call he had approved the final elements of the plan - and sanctioned some additional funding. Not that Sum Taeyoung had told him everything. Still Sum kept the final moves of his plot close to his chest. Now Viktor reached for his phone again and called his three comrades in arms, inviting the former Chekist fighters to a special celebratory tea party to coincide with Sum's Shah Mat date. They should, he told them, be together for the final move of their concluding game. Finally, he phoned the funding source for the whole plot, their patron, the Oligarch. In the briefest of conversations, the Russian oil tycoon expressed that he was well satisfied with events.

In California, Governor Al Williams stabbed at his computer in frustration and annoyance and cancelled yet another version of the script for his monumental and historic speech. His emotions were running high, a mixture of tenacious determination mixed with considerable foreboding. He was excited and nervous, inspired but massively apprehensive. He was, after all, simultaneously creating history but also stepping firmly into the unknown. With events now beyond his control and sailing forward like an unstoppable supertanker, he tried to cast aside doubts about his decisions, nagging inner worries as to the strength and capability of his own abilities, and concerns about his future. His fate was now in the lap of the Gods - or to be more precise - the Chinese. Or so he thought.

In one of the military wards of the QE Hospital in Birmingham, Nagriza Karimov fought for her life while Gene Bond paced the corridors nearby, sick with worry. The assassin's bullet had hit her in the chest, above her heart, and passed straight through her. There had been serious internal bleeding which had been the cause of the medical team's initial concerns. Now they had stabilised her but continued to be unsure of the ultimate outcome. It was still touch and go one of the medics told Bond.

Bond was having difficulty in clearing his mind of what had happened in his house the night before the shooting. She had been magnificent. Unselfish in their love making. Skilled. Gentle. And so passionate - so hungry. He felt as if he could still smell her - still taste her - still sense the warmness and raw nakedness of her body - her whimpering passiveness - her aggressive assertiveness. And there was the extraordinary coincidence of the Aral Sea. He felt closeness to her, a compassion for her past. But round and round his head circulated a persistent question. Was it just another 'convenience' to her, as with Georgi as she had confessed? Or was there more to it than that? Certainly Nagriza had made a huge impact on him, had really got under his skin. He felt devoted and caring towards her, but had no idea how she felt about him. He had only known her for the shortest of time yet she had quickly become a huge part of his life. He agonised over the prospect of losing her, despite the unsecure nature of their relationship.

On the outskirts of Birmingham, Georgi and Jamie took control of the old builders' yard as soon as they arrived, documented authority substantiated by appropriate messages from high places making it quickly evident to the many police on the scene that these two strangers from London would now be in charge of everything.

Bond had indeed killed the gunman whose corpse lay where the man had been felled by Bond's improvised weapon. The body and the man's clothing and his bag were thoroughly searched for any clues as to who he was. To the surprise of nobody, nothing was found. Georgi set a global search in motion for the man who looked to be European and whose equipment and style of operation indicated some sort of military background. Mechanisms were instigated to try and trace the history of both the rifle and hand gun. The numerous police who had already started their own investigations by the time Georgi and Jamie arrived, were now mere spectators and acting in support of Georgi.

In Wapping, in the basement of the former spice warehouses, Alan and Jane continued the struggle to decipher the chess game, now working on Jane's idea and translating the Russian text into South Korean Hangul. They considered themselves to be more than fortunate that they were dealing with the Revised Romanised version of the language and not the Asiatic hieroglyphic one. Even with computer help, progress was slow. They had, as agreed, focussed on the last square the Black Queen had landed on in her high speed progress across the chess board. The result of their labours was a confusion of letters. It was some hours before Jane achieved their second major breakthrough.

"Hey - how about this!" She thumped her desk in triumph. "I think some of these translate into numbers. They're not all letters." She paused briefly then added quizzically "It's just a case of which ones."

And with that in mind they ran various computer options and permutations before hitting a result that seemed to have some credibility. The answer was two sets of letters - AW and MMCC - and a set of numbers.

"Who or what or where is something with the initials AW and MMCC that Sum Taeyoung has been involved with, directly or indirectly?"

It took them less than half an hour of cross checking to find the answer- Al Williams, at the Montreux Music and Convention Centre, with the numbers translating to the date of the day after the DESA Summit had ended.

"OK," said Alan, excited and relieved by their progress at last. "So that's the last move of the Black Queen. What we think seems logical - apart from one thing. I don't understand why the numbers relate to the day after the DESA conference has ended. It would seem much more likely that any last move would correspond to the last day - or for that matter, any other day of the conference. The first day or the last day would seem to be the most significant. And because the Governor is making his speech on the last one, that's the one you would think to be the important one. So, why the day after the last day?"

"Agreed," responded Jane. "That's odd. You'd think with all those delegates from all over the world assembled in the Convention Centre, that would be the ideal opportunity for Taeyoung. A great platform, an international audience and the world's media all there. So why the day after? What's the significance? Can we find out if anything's scheduled to happen after the conference is ended? And until we do, I think we need to keep our guard up in regard to any of the conference days, but especially the last when Al Williams is speaking."

"OK," said Alan. "Let's do that. But if our general principle is right and the Black Queen relates to Al Williams, can we find a set of actions in which the Governor has been involved over a period of time and which might translate to the other squares the Black Queen has visited on her progress across the board? Maybe that'll help us understand what this plan is about. And maybe now the most important square to figure out is the next to last one. Maybe each square has some sort of action and date against it. Maybe this is what the chess game is - a schedule of actions and timings that culminate in the Governor being in Montreux on the last day of the DESA Summit - and doing something that has high significant the day after. But the big question then is - what?"

Jane agreed. "You keep working on this while I phone Georgi and update him. He needs to know what we now know."

Chapter 20

Ever cautious, ever the plotter and with the game moving towards its crescendo, Sum Taeyoung implemented some well planned, precautionary arrangements. While still in London he visited a young Englishman with a big reputation about anything to do with electronic surveillance. He spent half a day with him, exploring, testing, rejecting and accepting a number of optional actions, some of which they were able to undertake there and then. These included diversionary computer based activities that would take surveillance operatives or even hackers down long and complex cul de sacs to nowhere, and complex information loops that could send people running round and round in endless loops. The young Englishman produced a new and extremely expensive item from his portfolio of goodies - a digital image scrambler that interrupted and confused incoming signals and negated sophisticated computer systems that could search for individuals on the planet.

Apart from this highly technical, computer based activity, Sum also turned his attention to his physical appearance. The beard was removed. His head of hair was cut back to be almost a shadow on his head. He acquired medication to help him on a crash course of weight loss. Sum was fairly confident he could now shake off anyone taking too much interest in him. Using false identification, Sum eventually returned to Seoul, not directly but via Tokyo so as to complicate the trail for anyone who happened to be looking for him. On arrival back in the South Korean capital, he took more devious routes, not to his normal haunt but to another location he had had established some time ago more or less as a home though he rarely visited it. It was his personal hideaway, well equipped and with all the defensive mechanisms of the SDBI offices. But this was Sum's own domain, known to nobody. His theory was that if he needed to keep a low profile for a while, where better than in one of the world's biggest and busiest metropolises and his home city where personal connections were close to hand.

From here he set other activity into motion. He commissioned a world leading forger to undertake a particular piece of work. It would be a key part of the crescendo moment of his Shah Mat. Through his web of connections, he found which hotel the Governor would be staying at in Montreux and a timetable of his planned movements. He organised a freelance, three-man, ex-Russian army marine terrorist team into Switzerland and confirmed to them their role - a quite complex matter to achieve and very specific. They would come into play only at the very moment of the Shah Mat. He instructed Jake and Jo - already on their way to Montreux - to send an invitation to the Governor to attend a celebration party the day after his historic unilateral declaration of independence for California. The special enticement to the Governor was the spicing of the invitation with a promise that one of the senior Chinese officials behind the APTI oil deal would be attending but would not, for political reasons, be at the conference.

He had already made arrangements to hire one of Switzerland's historic steam paddle boats for the celebration party after the conference. He had a professional event planner putting all the arrangements together for what looked like a legitimate 'Party on the Lake' as he had insisted it be called. And via phone and email with the Event Manager, the timings of the event were drawn up in precise detail, from when invitations would be extended and to whom, to the time of boarding the boat, the drinks reception, the arrival of the American party, the buffet lunch, and the formal pinnacle moment of the event, a presentation to Governor Williams.

By the time these tasks were complete, Sum was content that the plot was in order and waterproof. But of growing concern to Sum was lack of news from the assassin he had hired in the UK. He expected by now to have had confirmation that the assignment had been fulfilled. The silence was disturbing.

Chapter 21

Georgi took the call from Jane and immediately headed into Birmingham, leaving the final elements of the killing site clean up to Jamie. The news from Wapping showed some real progress and significant breakthrough but highlighted the frustrations of still guessing what the end of the chess game really meant. They now knew it was to be in Montreux, to involve Governor Williams and, they suspected, to be on the day after the DESA conference ended. But precisely what it was still remained a total mystery.

On reaching the Queen Elizabeth Hospital Georgi tracked down Bond. News on Nagriza was still bleak but she continued to hold her own though remained on the critical list. Bond looked drawn and grey. It was very apparent to Georgi how much Nagriza had come to mean to Bond and though that puzzled him a little, he had too much on his mind to worry about that for now.

They sat in a coffee bar and exchanged news. Bond had little to say except to relay what he had been told by the medics who were treating Nagriza. Georgi updated Bond about the scene of the shooting on the outskirts of Birmingham and confirmed to Bond he had killed the gunman. Bond was horrified. He had never really physically harmed anyone before, let alone killed someone. The thought was horrendous to him and was diametrically opposed to his almost pacifist beliefs. He also worried about the consequences. He was horrified by the thought of appearing in court and having to defend his action. It took Georgi a long time to placate his friend and reassure him he had had no option but to do what he had done, that there would be no court case because this was no longer a police matter but something related to national security - and especially because he had been protecting Nagriza. He also reported to Bond that there was still no news as to who the gunman was.

Bond was in a very sober and reflective mood. "All this is so very alien to me," he told Georgi. "It may be your world and Nagriza's but it certainly isn't mine. I've never been shot at in my life and never thought I would be. And to kill someone - my God! To end a life! Whoever he was, he was still flesh and blood and a human being - with parents. Maybe family. And I killed him! It's sickening. It's unbelievable."

"You had no choice," Georgi insisted. "It was him or Nagriza. Or maybe both of you. In our world you can't afford to think beyond kill or be killed."

"But that's your world. It's not mine," responded Bond.

"It's the world of 007," Georgi responded and immediately wished he had not done so.

"Piss of Georgi! You know what I think about my name. I didn't choose it. I have nothing in common with Fleming's character. It's a bad joke. Especially at the moment. All this just because I was in the wrong pub in Scotland at the wrong time. And it's not as if I haven't got enough challenges in my own world. We've talked about some of them but there's another, practical side to all of this. While I'm dashing around the place dodging bullets and killing people, I'm not earning. While all of this has been going on I've lost sight of stuff I'm supposed to be working on - stuff that earns money for me apart from anything else. And that will damage my long term prospects. If you're not continuously visible in my world people soon forget you. And if you don't deliver what you've committed to deliver, you don't get paid. Now I've been sucked into a world that I didn't know existed and one that has got nothing to do with me."

There was a silence between them. It was a while before Georgi responded.

"But, my friend, it has so much to do with you and what you're trying to do. Strangely enough, the legitimate side of SDBI and what Sum Taeyoung does is plumb on your agenda. The trouble is, he's mixed it up with a totally different agenda, and that's why you're where you are now."

Bond thought about that for a while and was about to respond when Georgi added: "And whether you like it or not, you're in this up to your neck and you've got to see it through."

Bond nodded slowly and looked Georgi firmly in the eyes.

"I know. I know I've no choice now. But this is not my world. I don't recognise it. I don't like its values. It frightens the shit out of me - and I don't like seeing people get hurt - even if they're trying to hurt me. You might not be able to understand that but that's the way I am. But I will see it through to the end, whatever that is. I just have to now."

Again a silence dropped between them, both wrapped in their own thoughts. Eventually Georgi felt he had to move them out of this reflective mode and back to the issues at hand.

And he told Bond what Jane had reported from Wapping.

"Clearly Sum Taeyoung's plot peaks at some moment of glory for him which seems to be on the day after the DESA conference. We've no idea what that is and we're still worried we've got the timing right. It seems so odd that Taeyoung's big moment isn't going to be in the conference itself. But whatever it is and whenever it is, it wont be good news for anyone except Sum Taeyoung, we can be sure about that. I don't know whether it's to do with something that will happen to the Governor, or something to do with the oil deal. But it seems to me very doubtful that Sum is hugely bothered one way or another about the Governor. He's just a pawn in this chess game. As far as I know, Al Williams still has no awareness of Sum Taeyoung's plotting or even existence. So that narrows it down to the oil deal. But what about the oil deal? I don't know. I had thought about trying to tell him - but what do I tell him? I can't even prove the link between APTI and SDBI. And he would have no idea who I am - someone he doesn't know from an organisation that doesn't exist! Some chance him listening to me."

"I know him," said Bond.

"Shit," responded Georgi, amazed. "That's something that never crossed my mind. Now my friend, it's you who has the surprises."

"It's a bit of an exaggeration to say I know him," explained Bond. "We've met once. He came to the UK a couple of years ago to speak at an environmental conference. I was keen to meet him to find out direct from him about Californian activity on sustainable development. The State has always been a forward thinker about environmental stuff. I had about an hour with him over a lunch. It was the only slot in his diary and I was surprised he agreed to give me some time. But he did. I thought we got on well."

"Would he remember you?" asked Georgi.

"I've no idea," Bond responded. "He might. But if I sent him an email or tried to phone him I guess I would only get to him via the usual bureaucratic and slow channels. There'll be a ring of protection around him and I doubt I could get through that. I certainly wouldn't guarantee it."

Georgi thought about that for a while.

"Would he recognise you?"

"I guess so," answered Bond. "But I couldn't guarantee that either."

Again a pause for thought from Georgi.

"But if he did recognise you - if you could get in front of him - he might listen. These are mighty big ifs and mights. But it could be a chance."

"What are you suggesting?" asked Bond.

"I've no bloody idea," responded Georgi. "I'm making this up as we talk."

Another pause.

"I think we've got to go to Montreux," announced Georgi finally. "There's no option. It's the only move we can make. We've got to try and get you in front of the Governor so you can tell him what we know. I agree that's not a lot, but I think it's the only chance we have."

"When would we have to go?" asked Bond.

"Now," said Georgi with a look that spelt determination. "The DESA conference starts tomorrow, Wednesday. I think Al Williams flies in there on Thursday. He has a day with the conference and UN people before he makes his speech when the conference closes Friday. He's the final big act in the programme. So Saturday is the day after the last day of the DESA event - and the date of the last square on the chess game. We've got to get to him before then - and I guess before he makes his speech. If we organise it now we could travel tomorrow, spend Thursday trying to get at the Governor before he gives his speech Friday."

"You'd try and stop him making the speech?" asked Bond.

Georgi laughed dryly at the suggestion. "I don't think that's realistic. What reason do I have to stop him? We have a load of unsubstantiated stuff and absolutely no authority. But clearly something's going to happen there and if we're able to forewarn him maybe we can prevent it."

"But we don't know what we're looking for," said Bond, clearly not enthused by this idea.

"So what? We've been grovelling in the dark ever since you and I met in the Russian bar and you told me your story. I guess the truth is you've been in the dark ever since that shooting in Scotland."

Bond was surprised to realise he had not thought about the incident in Scotland for some time. The shooting in Scotland had been the most terrible thing Bond had ever been involved in - up to then. But since that bloody incident so many other things had happened it had been overtaken by events and become an almost lost memory.

"What about Nagriza?" asked Bond. "We can't just leave her here."

"Yes we can," replied Georgi firmly. "We can't move her. We can't do anything to help her. She's no idea what's happening in the world so she doesn't know if we're here or if we're not here. She has the best medical support we could hope for. So truly, there's nothing more we can do for her just now. And if the Governor recognises you it has to be you that goes to Montreux. I need to go with you to try and find out what Sum's up to and what he's plotting in Montreux and to try and stop it. So we have to go, my friend. And anyway the truth is, as I keep stressing, there's nothing you can do here. And professionally, Nagriza would cut your balls off if she knew you'd refused to go so you could stay by her side - while she slept and knew nothing about anything."

Bond remained hugely unhappy about the plan and argued against it. But even as he did so he knew it was a forlorn battle with Georgi, and one he eventually lost.

Some quick calls by Georgi, including to the team in Wapping, ascertained that the fastest and confirmed available way the two of them could get to Montreux was via a flight out of Manchester early the next day, taking them to Geneva and then by train down to Montreux with a quick train change at Lausanne. Bond, still cursing that the Porsche was stuck in Scotland, hired a car to get them to

Manchester in the morning, the two resting the night at Bond's house where Jamie also stayed.

The journey to Switzerland and its beautiful and famous lake was uneventful but time consuming, frustrating and tedious. The only bonus was the train journey from Geneva which largely runs alongside the lake and gave them stunning views of classic Alpine scenery. On a gloriously sunny day, Lake Geneva looked crystal and blue, surrounded by the imposing mountains with their high and white tops. By the time they reached Montreux it was late afternoon and the first day of the DESA conference was winding down to its end.

With the UN event in town, trying to find accommodation had been a nightmare but in the end they were lucky with some delegates not turning up and a couple of rooms becoming available in the Grand Hotel, conveniently almost opposite the railway station and a five minute taxi drive down the hill to the lakeside and the Music and Convention Centre. Having established themselves in their rooms, they met in the bar to develop a battle plan.

"We've got this evening, tomorrow and the last day of the conference on Friday. Then there's Saturday, seemingly crunch day on Taeyoung's plan," Georgi told Bond. "Al Williams is basically in two places during that time, the Convention Centre or his hotel. Apart from Saturday, that is. Then we don't know what's happening. I wish we did!"

"He's staying at the Majestic," Bond said.

"How do you know that?" asked Georgi.

"I asked in the lobby," Bond replied. "Everyone seems to know. The Majestic's down the hill, on the same road as the Convention Centre."

Georgi thought for a while and was then decisive about their action plan. "OK, there's not much we can do with great impact until Al Williams arrives tomorrow, and we don't know what time that will be. I suggest tomorrow you go to the Majestic. Hang around in the lobby. Try and find out what time Al Williams is scheduled to arrive. Ideally, when he walks into the hotel you could try and intercept him and speak to him. Hopefully he'll recognise you. While you're there, see if you can find out what his movements are for the rest of his visit. We need to find that moment to get you in front of him if it doesn't work in the hotel lobby. We can't count on that. It's a very long shot. But you'll have to be careful. There's bound to be security people there. If you're too obviously overly curious you might end up in trouble. Don't do that."

"Meantime, for what's left of today, I suggest you go down to the Majestic and see what else you can find out. But be discreet. I'll go down to the Convention Centre and test the security there. I'm getting some papers sent over electronically from Wapping. They should be here soon. I hope they'll give me some authority - but I doubt it. It depends what organisation I can purport to be from that has any clout around here."

So they split up.

Chapter 22

The Miles Davis Hall is named after the famed American jazz and rock and roll musician. It also helps denote that it is the home every year to the internationally respected Montreux Jazz Festival. This part of the Montreux Music and Convention Centre where the UN event was to be held is entered by a fairly nondescript side entrance located on the short section of road that climbs steeply uphill from the direction of Lake Geneva to a junction with the Rue du Lac, the hardly adventurously named main road that runs through the lower parts of Montreux. The entrance to the Miles Davis Hall is at that junction.

As Georgi approached it he found the whole area had been cordoned off with police and military people in large numbers and a police tape clearly showing where unauthorised people could now no longer go. Numerous uniformed men and a few uniformed women stood around and a number of military vehicles were parked in the road and down on the path running alongside the Lake and in front of the Convention Centre. For locals and tourists alike it was a serious and infuriating inconvenience and an intrusion into their normally tranquil lifestyles. To Georgi it was an enormous frustration. Even the flashing of his newly arrived credentials and the support letters from the UK Foreign Office that he had brought out with him did nothing. He was referred from one person in authority to another then another until he became both utterly frustrated and increasingly worried that his persistence might draw unwanted attention.

He found he could not get close to the building from any direction. In effect it was cut off from the lakeside and the main road had been closed causing traffic chaos as through traffic was diverted to the narrower roads of the main part of town, higher up the hill. While on land the four sides of the Centre were sealed off, in the dying light of the day as evening started to turn into night, Georgi spotted that out on the lake itself some rigid ribbed inflatables were growling around with their rasping, high powered engines, obviously patrolling the waters offshore from the Centre. The cordon was complete. Georgi would not have expected it to be otherwise. His futile efforts finally thwarted, a somewhat exasperated Georgi headed back up the hill. To add to his frustration, the only taxis he saw were occupied and he eventually resigned himself to having to walk.

Bond meantime had settled into a comfortable chair on the ground floor level of the Majestic. This was his trial run to see whether there was any real potential of intercepting Al Williams here. The idea of sitting in the hotel lobby watching the world go by and hoping to catch a moment with the Governor proved easier in theory than in practice. The Majestic has no discernable lobby but a very large area in which the entrance from the front door and the long reception desk are part of a ground floor complex of several raised floor levels, discreet seating areas and an open link to an adjacent restaurant. The best he could do was establish himself in a lounge chair where he could keep an eye on the front door and pretend to read a copy of yesterday's New York Times that he had picked up from a rack of international newspapers. He kept a wary eye on the flow of people that was constantly moving in and out of the hotel and eventually was able to recognise the half a dozen well built, suited men who wandered around with seemingly nothing really to do and nowhere to go to. Twice since he established himself in his chair he had been approached and asked who he was and what he was doing. Twice he had replied that he was waiting for a guest. Fortunately nobody tested him further because if they had he would have struggled to find answers. But the response he gave was half true and gave him some seemingly slim legitimacy for being where he was. No effort was made to move him on though he was conscious of the guarded glimpses towards him every now and then from the suited brigade. He felt he was on borrowed time and that eventually he would be asked to leave - or worse. He felt uncomfortable and nervous.

With the conference coming to the end of its first day, the hotel that had been quiet when he had arrived with just a few delegates, officials and security people milling around, was now becoming busier. Clearly some delegates had left the conference before its close and the buzz of chatter around the hotel was getting louder. By eavesdropping on a few conversations and hearing the odd word or two as people walked by, Bond was eventually able to store two pieces of information. Al Williams was definitely due in tomorrow - about midday. He would arrive from

Geneva by helicopter and by limo for the final stages of the journey into the town centre and to the hotel. He was due to speak at the conference the next day, Friday, in the mid afternoon. He would leave the hotel around eleven o'clock to take lunch at the Convention Centre but it was unclear what the Governor would be doing in the early morning. Polishing up his speech, Bond surmised. There was no clue as to what might happen on Saturday.

He and Georgi met back in their hotel for evening dinner and swapped what information they had.

"Tomorrow and Friday are our last chances," Georgi said. "We must do everything we can to make contact with Al Williams. You try him at the hotel. I'll see what else we might do - see what Wapping might be able to pull. I wish to God we knew more about Sum's intentions for Saturday."

After a light meal they retired to their respective beds where Bond spent a restless night thinking about the coming days - and about Nagriza.

Thursday proved a futile and frustrating day for the two of them. Despite Georgi's best diplomatic and string pulling efforts he got nowhere in breaking through the bureaucratic wall surrounding the Governor. Bond, having felt uncomfortable hanging around Al Williams' hotel the previous day and thinking people would recall he had done that, killed time on through the morning and only moved to The Majestic at midday. The general expectations were that Al Williams would arrive at 1300. By then Bond had got himself into the best position he could. But all his efforts were badly rewarded when Williams and his entourage swept through the hotel at high speed, from door to elevator in seemingly seconds and with numerous hefty men keeping tight formation around him. Governor Williams was gone in a speedy blur and Bond stood rooted where he was, utterly thwarted, his hopes shattered.

In fact, Governor Williams had caught a fleeting glimpse of Bond in the hotel lobby and had recognised him instantly and recalled their meeting in the past. But it had been a mere glimpse and not enough for him to divert away from his planned programme.

Now Al Williams reached his suite of rooms, his base until Saturday afternoon. Thanking his PPS and the attending team, he shut the door behind him and gave a big sigh. It had been a testing journey from the USA. Now all he wanted was a little peace and tranquillity - some space of his own - and a drink.

"God is on my side - or at least for a little while," he thought to himself as he found to his delight a bottle of Bourbon had thoughtfully been left for him. He poured a stiff measure onto ice rocks and walked over to the large double window that overlooked the lake. He found he could open it and walk onto a balcony which provided a spectacular view of the lake and its surrounding mountains. He took huge and numerous deep intakes of the stunningly clean air, such a refreshing contrast to the artificial air of the aircraft, the limousine and the hotel. He sank into a comfortable lounger.

His mind was full of the next day and his moment in the spotlight of history. After all his years in politics and despite his maturing years, events had taken Al Williams into a set of circumstances he could never have envisaged or really, if he was truly honest with himself, wanted. And though he had led from the front as he felt was the responsibility of his role, deep within himself niggled a set of doubts as to his ability to deliver what was being asked of him, not just in the speech and what that meant, but in the actual taking of California into independence. It was a monumental ambition. Williams was a popular politician - at the moment - largely because he consistently demonstrated strong leadership, something the Californian electorate appreciated.

But while that might be his image to the outside world, Williams had his private self doubts that normally remained as mere shadows deep within him. But now, as he sat and sipped his iced Bourbon, he realised those uncertainties had risen from the shadows and were now increasingly playing big time on his mind. It was, he told himself sternly, something he must control.

"The more you think about them the more the doubts will grow and eventually they'll win," he muttered into his whisky glass with its golden content, trying to shake himself into a more positive mood.

As a way of helping that, he returned indoors and went to his laptop that had already been set up for him. He spent half an hour checking messages and responding to some of them. It was enough to get him into a work mode and his brain thinking and, having achieved that, he opened the files on his computer where tomorrow's speech was in draft form.

He had spent an age working on the speech in its current form. Internal advisors had provided their input as had some specifically chosen external ones. Now, he felt, at last, he could shape and fashion the script to his own liking, unrestricted by anyone. He was committed to ensuring the presentation sounded like it was coming from him as an honest, passionate and deeply committed individual rather than giving the impression he was reading the words on behalf of some obscure committee.

But it was the tone of the delivery that concerned him the most. The fundamental detail and statutory elements had long since been set in concrete, mainly based on the input of constitutional lawyers. Al Williams' worries now were that he presented this history making speech in a statesman like style, with authority, honesty and integrity but without signs of arrogance or victory over those who had opposed the move.

And, as he did with such scripts, he read it out loud. Experience had taught him that words spoken in the mind often sound very different to when they are communicated externally to an audience. So he stood by his computer and read the words off the screen in a style he would use tomorrow when standing at a lectern in front of an audience of some 400 delegates and the world's media.

"Our forefathers," he said "who wrote the American Constitution did so with certain principles uppermost in their minds. But the underlying principle is one that is concerned about people power."

He marked on the computer script a large, red, upper case P. Again it was experience at play. He knew the power of the pause but also how easy it was to forget that in the pressurised moment of giving a presentation. So, as had become his habit, he marked the script with red Ps where he felt a pause would give emphasis. He also wrote in red the word SLOW every now and then as it was his habit to speak faster and faster as a speech progressed and his enthusiasm and confidence grew.

"The only legitimate constitution is one that originates with, and is controlled by, the people. It is more than just a set of rules."

"As the Anglo-American political activist, author, political theorist and revolutionary Thomas Paine said way back in the 1700's - 'A constitution is not the act of a government, but of a *people* constituting a government, and a government without a constitution is power without right.' This remains as the backbone of our Constitution that says the Constitution is ordained and established not by the government but by 'We the People'."

Another red P. Perhaps, if he was lucky, the pause might also be in response to applause.

"For more than 300 years the Constitution has stood us in good stead. In fact, I contend it still does. There are, however, two contemporary problems that interfere with this. One is the loss of applied appropriate governance by today's custodians of the Constitution who seem to have forgotten that they act and manage the Constitution on behalf of the people, not on behalf of the government. And the second is the sheer size of the monster that the United States has become that makes the link between the people and the administrators of Government sometimes so tenuous as to disenfranchise the majority of the people from the very administration that is supposed to be governing them."

Another red P.

"That is why turnout at elections has dwindled. People no longer feel they can influence a political mechanism from which they feel distanced and isolated. So they don't bother to vote. Voting numbers have dropped to dangerous levels when the number of people turning out to vote is very small, not representative, and vulnerable to the manipulations of extreme political groups."

And as the speech developed he focused on issues to do with the challenges and practicalities of delivering democratic politics in a modern, fast moving, sophisticated world. The speech would last 45 minutes. It was only when he reviewed it he realised that the issue of oil from China was mentioned only once in a section that took just under five minutes. It was virtually a passing comment and that made it even clearer to him that the deal he had signed with China had not been the main reason for the success of the Referendum in sparking the breakaway of California from the United States of America. It had just been a spark-point to what, eventually, was going to be inevitable anyway, sometime.

Chapter 23

Thursday evening, like the rest of the day when they assessed it later, had been more or less a write off. There was, in essence, nothing to put down in any column marked 'achieved'.

There was almost total silence between them during dinner which neither of them felt any appetite for. Later, back in Georgi's room, Georgi was in a sulky mood which Bond had never seen before. His Georgian friend roamed around the room, muttering what Bond assumed to be expletives in his mother tongue, sitting every now and then but only briefly before continuing to roam like a bear with a bad headache.

"I hate this," he grunted to Bond in frustration. "This - this - inaction. This - where we are not in control of events, where we don't even know what the events to come are - when we don't know what to prepare for - what to look for. It's shit!"

And Bond watched with some concern as a fairly regular flow of red wine disappeared down Georgi's gullet.

"If we don't know what shit is going to happen - or even when - how the hell can we plan to counter it?"

And the Georgian had wandered meaninglessly around the room again, sometimes stopping to gaze wistfully out of the window as if he might somehow see inspirational answers to his questions in the lake or the mountains.

Finally, preceded by an explosion of Georgian expletives, Georgi announced his intentions.

"I can't stand this anymore. Sum has the upper hand because he knows what's going to happen. And when. We don't. It's like working in a dark tunnel. And, we're running out of time. We know Sum's action - whatever he's planned - is scheduled soon. Saturday maybe. Tomorrow perhaps. It's Thursday night now and we have no idea what he's up to. Time is running out!"

He banged his fist against the back of a chair.

"In the morning, when the conference has started, I'm going to do a little - what you call - poking around."

"What do you mean?" Bond was getting worried now. Was alcohol fuelling this new bravado or was it sensible tactics?

"How the hell do I know?" Georgi spat back. "I'm still making this crap up as I go along. But I can't stand this lack of action. So I make my own action. Tomorrow morning I'm going to, er," he stumbled for the right English words as his speech got increasingly excited. "To have a search around Al Williams' room. See if that shines any light into our black tunnel."

"You've got to be joking," retorted Bond.

"No. No joke my friend. Just to make some action happen."

"What good will that do?" queried Bond.

"Fuck knows," fired back Georgi. "But I've got to do something. If you have any better ideas, you tell me." His tone was aggressive - challenging.

"And what can I do?" asked Bond, accepting that there was no way he could counter what Georgi now planned to do.

"Whatever you want," came a disparagingly throw away reply. "Why not keep trying to get in front of Williams. That's the one thing you might do that nobody else can do."

And with that they split up and retired for the night.

Georgi slept later than he had intended, missing breakfast at a decent hour so deciding to miss it altogether. By the time he was showered, dressed and kitted out for some sort of espionage-like action, the conference was well into the start of its final, historic day and it was pushing towards lunchtime. Georgi kept checking his watch, counting down the time to noon Saturday. They had roughly 24 hours left! That is, if Sum Taeyoung's plot was to be revealed at 1200 Saturday. But Georgi, like Jane, still worried that Sum's target would be Al Williams as he spoke to the UN assembly that afternoon. There was a slight feeling of panic within him which his experience would normally control. Strangely, this time, it was growing within him and would not go away. It annoyed him intensely, adding to his agitation. Sum Taeyoung was getting to him. Getting under his skin.

He was just about to leave his room when his mobile phone rang. It was Jane, calling on a secure line from Wapping.

"I don't know if this is going to help," she said. "But we've made some progress on breaking through the chess game code."

She notably did not mention Sum or Al Williams because though the line was supposed to be safe, there was always concern it was not one hundred per cent so.

"I'll tell you afterwards how we've got this far but we seem to have found that on Saturday our number one man is inviting the star performer to something called 'A Party On The Lake'. There's nothing else but I thought you should know. Maybe it does shift the attention away from this afternoon."

"Maybe," responded Georgi, still not convinced despite this new development. He decided against telling her what he planned to do in the immediate future. He knew she would be as unenthusiastic as Bond. Instead, he thanked her for the call, picked up his holdall and left the hotel.

He found the Majestic Hotel quiet with few people about. Those attending the conference had long since gone and it seemed the security people had left with the Governor. At least, there was no sign of them in the lobby. Georgi was surprised about that but it was a bonus. He already knew which floor Al Williams' rooms were on. He crossed the entrance hall to the elevators and took one to the floor above where Al Williams' room was. The elevators were accessed in central areas in the corridors of each floor. Not being too sure of the layout, Georgi arbitrarily chose to turn left as he exited onto the floor and strode purposefully towards the end of the corridor and a door that was shut. He was acutely conscious that CCTV cameras were everywhere and if he was not being monitored now he would surely be seen when people checked tapes later, as they might.

He had been concerned that the door he was heading towards would lead through to some sort of service area where his presence would have been more conspicuous and open to challenge. But as he got closer he became increasingly confident that it was not just a service door and he was relieved when he pushed it open to find he was in a stairwell, carpeted and with pictures on the walls. Clearly this was somewhere open to hotel guests which made his presence far easier to explain than if it had been an area restricted to staff only. A quick pause for a look around told him that, contrary to other parts of the hotel, there was not a surveillance camera to be seen. He hurried down the stairs to the floor where Al Williams' rooms were. Rather than burst through the door and into the corridor, Georgi took his phone from his pocket, opened the door a little, and used the highly polished back of the phone as a mirror to look down the corridor.

Bond had commented on Georgi's phone in the past. Its polished back was very unusual, prompting Bond to call Georgi a "decadent Eastern European hypocrite."

"Western chauvinist," Georgi had retorted. "And what about your Porsche? Hardly the choice of transport for a green conservationist! Don't you call me a hypocrite!"

But the glazed rear of Georgi's phone was designed to fit exactly the purpose he was now putting it to and which, through its mirrored surface, enabled him to see that there was one person in the corridor. By the door to Al Williams' room stood a tall young coloured man with short cropped hair, well dressed in an expensive, lightweight striped suit. From his posture and mannerisms, Georgi immediately took him to be either military or police. In either case, it did not matter. It was to be expected.

Self doubts about his own 'make it up as you go along' plan of the evening before, fuelled as they had been by copious amounts of wine, started to take hold of Georgi. Maybe, he thought, this was not a good idea after all. And with that running round his mind, he caught the elevator down to the ground level again, intent on having a cool, non-alcoholic drink to help him sort his mind out a little, take stock of the situation and review his plan, what there was of it.

But, every now and then, fate plays unexpected cards. When the elevator reached ground level, the doors opened and there stood a bellhop, silver tray in hand. In a flash Georgi saw an opportunity! The man was about his size and on the plate was an envelope with the name Al Williams on it. In the bat of an eye Georgi responded to fate and, in a strong foreign accent of no discernable national origin but in English, said to the man before him, "sorry, wrong floor." And instead of exiting the elevator, with a nod of apology to the bellhop, he stepped back into it. The bellhop pushed the button to send the elevator up to Al Williams' floor.

By the time they got there the bellhop was unconscious and pushed into a corner. The elevator stopped briefly and then continued up again on Georgi's further command. He prayed for some luck and that nobody else would try to use the elevator while he put the bellhop's jacket on and took a small device from within his holdall. It looked like a miniature travel clock. He had positioned the clock and set it by the time the elevator was back at Al Williams' floor.

Exiting the elevator but pushing a button to send it and the unconscious bellhop back up again as he did so, he nonchalantly dropped his own jacket on a chair so he could retrieve it later. He had taken only a couple of steps along the corridor when he heard a somewhat dull and only just distinguishable 'thump' as his small but effective explosive device stopped the elevator between floors. He headed off towards the man he had seen earlier in his phone mirror who now looked up from the paper he was reading. He studied Georgi as he walked towards him. Georgi recognised all the signs. This was a trained reaction. A SWOT analysis of risk. He was looking to see how Georgi walked - normally or in a pre-combatant way with muscles tensed and balance such that the body could spring quickly one way or another. Was there sign of a weapon? Was the envelope tray what it seemed to be?

Within a few feet of him Georgi extended his arm as if to give the man the envelope on the tray. Instinctively, the man reached for it but as his hand closed towards the tray Georgi tilted it slightly so the envelope fell to the floor. In microseconds the other man had to make a judgement. Was that an accident or deliberate? To Georgi it did not matter now if he or the other man picked up the envelope. Whichever, it would present Georgi with the moment he needed. As it happened it was the other man who bent to pick it up, slowly and trying to keep his eye on Georgi all the time except for a split second when he momentarily looked to see where the envelope was resting on the floor. Having done so, and despite all his trained abilities to hopefully be wary of such moments and not to fall into any trap, that is just what happened. As he returned his eyes from the envelope back to Georgi, Georgi was waiting for him with a surprise.

"There is no way, my friend, that I will not use this if you force me to," Georgi told the man who was clearly aware of the pistol with its silencer now pointed at him but which Georgi concealed from the cameras by keeping it under the tray.

"Now open the door."

"You're making a big mistake friend," came an unmistakably Californian response.

"No, it is you who will make the mistake," promised Georgi. "Open the fucking door!"

The man hesitated, his eyes never off Georgi's. But whatever his thought processes, he obviously came to the conclusion that opening the door would at least buy him some time. So he opened it and they walked in, Georgi locking the door behind him.

"Sit over there," Georgi barked his instruction, nodding to a nearby chair. Georgi noted that the tall American was well balanced on his feet like a prize fighter coiled up and about to leap at his opponent. He responded very slowly and deliberately to Georgi's commands.

"Look," Georgi told him. "There's no way you're going to believe this but we're on the same side. Al Williams is in great danger and I am trying to keep him safe."

"Who the hell are you?" asked the man.

"I'm working with the authority of the European Union, the UK MI6 and the US SIS."

"So you say buddy. But what's your own unit? And show me some authority."

It was the response Georgi dreaded but expected.

"I can't do either I'm afraid. What authorisation I have you guys wouldn't recognise. There's nothing more I can say. So, I regret to tell you we are where we are. But, I'm the one with the gun, pointed at you. What I want you to do is very carefully put your own gun on the floor and kick it towards me."

Again the man's steely eyes caught Georgi's in a stare. A very fast assessment was going on. The options. The risks. The potential outcomes.

After a short delay, the man dropped his gaze and shuffled gently in his chair as, with the thumb and finger of his left hand, he pulled a gun from his jacket and dropped it to the floor. The kick was not that good and the gun ended up about half way between the two of them. It looked like the result of poor judgement, but it was not. They both knew it was not.

Georgi's next action was to open the letter that he had carried into the room on the silver platter. To his surprise it was from APTI. It read:

To Governor Al Williams of the Independent Nation of California

We would be honoured if you would join us on Saturday for a Party on the Lake to celebrate the historic declaration of independence by California. This will be a private and select event and will include representatives from the United Nations and the Government of the People's Republic of China. We will also be honoured if you will receive an Award to commemorate your presiding role in these momentous events.

We will board a Lake Steamer at 1030 from the landing stage by the Music and Convention Centre. The Presentation will be at 1200.

Your office and PPSs have been advised of this addition to your programme and it has been planned into a revised schedule for you.

It was signed by Jake Bloomer on behalf of ATPI. There was an r.s.v.p. request and a telephone number to respond to.

Georgi read the note twice before folding it up again and placing it back in the envelope. The message confirmed what Jane had told him but with a little more detail. Georgi had only just folded the letter and replaced it in the envelope when there was a knock at the door - an urgent and loud ratatat. A voice rang out. "My name is Captain John Starky of the US Military Police. I am here with six highly armed and experienced marines. I want you to throw down your handgun and allow my colleague to open this door. You have 10 seconds to respond."

Georgi looked at the Californian. The other man looked him straight back, eye to eye, and shrugged his shoulders. It was immediately clear to Georgi this man had somehow sent some sort of signal out of the room. It could only have been when he was removing his gun from his jacket.

"Sometimes you win. Sometimes you lose baby," said the man. "This time you lost fella - big time. Give it up like the man says."

Georgi kept his gun held straight at its target for several seconds before lowering it. In a flash the other man had retrieved his own gun, taken Georgi's from him and called to the armed team outside it was safe for them to enter. With a look of disrespect at Georgi, he went and unlocked the door to let his comrades in.

The man who had knocked on the door and called to Georgi walked in, unhurriedly and with authority. Behind him, six marines brought their rifles to bear on Georgi.

"On the deck," said the lead officer. Georgi did as he was instructed. He realised he was caught red handed and outgunned. There was no point in doing anything else but accept the situation.

As the lead man roughly pushed Georgi onto his front and bound his hands behind his back he said, "now, who the hell are you? What have we got here?"

Georgi knew he had made a colossal and unforgivable mistake. His impetuous actions were as foolhardy as Bond had warned they were. Now he was going to be out of the game. Bond would be on his own. With perhaps only something like 20 hours now left.

Chapter 24

Bond's useless efforts to get at Al Williams played on his mind all Thursday night. He had a sleepless night during which his brain would not stop working. He worried about when Sum Taeyoung might strike. Would it be Friday or Saturday? How could he get at Al Williams? What would Georgi achieve - or what damage might he do? Eventually, in the early hours of Friday morning as the sun started to rise over the mountains and light his hotel room, a new idea came to him. It rolled around his mind for a long time before he eventually gave up any hope of further sleep and left his bed to use some of the hotel's writing paper to write a note to Governor Williams.

Dear Governor Williams

My name is Gene Bond. I am an English environmental entrepreneur. We have met before when we had lunch together in London. I very much hope you will remember me.
I am currently in Montreux. The reason for me being here is that I believe your life is in immediate danger. I know this sounds preposterous and melodramatic but it is the truth. I urgently need to speak to you personally before tomorrow (Saturday) morning. I am now in the lobby of the Majestic Hotel, immediately available to see you at any time convenient to yourself. I will wait here in the hope of a positive response.

Gene Bond

After breakfast, unable to get any response from Georgi and therefore assuming he had already left the building, Bond walked down the hill to the Majestic Hotel. It was early and the morning rush hour was only just gaining a momentum. He had no way of knowing that Georgi had actually gone nowhere but was oversleeping with an unhealthy hangover. Bond felt a little better now he had a clear plan and a determination that he would successfully execute it.

His first port of call was the reception desk. There was a solitary man managing it. Annoyingly, because it was early, two guests of the hotel were checking out and Bond had to wait several frustrating minutes before it became his turn to be attended to. He was thankful the hotel was largely taken over by people at the UN event otherwise there might have been many more guests waiting to check out.

"I want to speak to the Duty Manager please," said Bond directly when the man behind the counter turned to him.

"I am sure I can be of service to you, sir. What do you require?" The words were in English but the origins were obviously very French. The integrity of the apparent respect being offered was very plastic and veneer thin as, Bond thought, is often the case with such people.

"I need to speak to the Duty Manager," Bond repeated.

"I'm sorry, sir. I insist that if you can tell me what you want, I will be able to help you."

Bond lent forward, glaring in determination. "Look. I need to see your Duty Manager - now. It's a matter of the utmost urgency. It's to do with Governor Williams. If I don't see your Duty Manager soon, the reason why I want to see him may be too late. I hope you are happy to take responsibility for the consequences because, believe me, I will ensure you do."

The man straightened his tie. "Oh, Governor Williams. Yes, sir. Just wait a minute please." And he turned and disappeared into the office area behind the reception desk. Bond could see him through the window speaking into a telephone. There was much gesticulation.

In just under four minutes the Duty Manager was at the front desk. He was much in the same mould of the man Bond had previously been speaking to. A bit more refined perhaps, more conceited and more sure of himself.

"Oh, Mr Bond. How pleasing to meet you. How can I be of assistance?" The pleasantries were gushing and nauseating. This man exuded all the characteristics of his trade that Bond despised - robotic like artificial politeness and transparent sincerity.

"Yes," replied Bond taking the enveloped note to Al Williams from his inside jacket pocket. "I need this note to be with Governor Williams at the earliest opportunity. And by that I mean now! I cannot stress enough to you the importance of its content. If it's subsequently found the message was delayed in its delivery, this hotel, its owners, and you especially will be held to account and in the most serious of difficulties. To put it as clearly as I can - you, personally, will be in the shit deeper than you would believe possible!"

The manager took the envelope from Bond and looked at it as if it were toxic.

"And it is my intention," Bond told him, "to take up position in the lobby area and await a response from the Governor. I know he is still in his room and I know that once he opens the envelope he will wish to see me."

It was a significant bluff by Bond. He really had no idea how Williams would respond. Indeed, despite what he had said, he did not even know if the Governor was in his room. But having set the challenge to the hotel, Bond left the reception desk and with an air of determination went and sat in a nearby comfortable chair. He had no sooner done so than a waiter arrived at his side.

"May I offer Mr Bond an aperitif - on behalf of the hotel?" He spoke in the softest of voices with a strong French accent.

Bond declined politely but felt the hotel must be taking him seriously for this extended hand of friendship - as he took it to be - to be forthcoming.

Ten minutes passed. Then another ten. Seeds of doubt started to take root in Bond's mind and he felt defeat starting to stare him in the face again. He had felt so positive about this way of getting to Williams. If this failed, what next? He was playing the only card he had got. It was just short of half an hour, with Bond on the verge of re-approaching the reception desk, when a very smartly dressed, mature woman approached him. She spoke to him with an aristocratic English accent.

"Mr Bond. I am Celia. I am a PPS to Governor Al Williams. I am here to extend an invitation for you to join the Governor for morning tea in his hotel room - now."

The last word was said firmly. So firmly it became a command rather than an invitation. Bond tingled with excitement mixed with a sense of enormous relief. His ploy had paid off! He could hardly believe it as he followed the tall and shapely form of Celia to the elevator and up to Al Williams' floor. On the short journey she said to him "I'm afraid this has to be quite quick. You will appreciate this is an historic day and Governor Williams has to leave for the Convention Centre in half an hour. We absolutely must be away from here by ten thirty. He has vetoed all calls and visitors so you are very much the exception."

"I understand - and am honoured," said Bond, overjoyed at the opportunity he was being granted, however short it was.

As they entered the Governor's room, Bond immediately caught site of Al Williams, surrounded by a group of people and in deep conversation, no doubt about the speech he was soon to make. Williams looked up and saw Bond enter.

"Gene! Gene! How good to see you again - and of course I recall our lunch in London. It is good to see you." He stressed the word "is" but immediately added "but this is not a good time for us to meet. Today of all days! But your note was intriguing and even alarming. What is it you want to tell me?"

"Can we talk about this in private, sir?" asked Bond moving forward to shake the Governor's hand who then guided him into a second room and closed the door behind him.

"Let me make it clear Gene that I hold you in great respect for the work you do," said Williams. "Otherwise you would not have seen me today. Today is a quite exceptional day, to understate the obvious! I am under great pressure and have no spare time in my schedule. But I could not ignore your note. It was dramatic - even theatrical and melodramatic. I would have dismissed it from most people. But, coming from you - that's different. What's on your mind?"

Bond had been dreading this moment. Clearly he was keen to tell the Governor what he knew, and to warn him of impending danger. But to drop a story of this magnitude and complexity on to anyone without any warning and to expect them to understand, take it seriously and respond immediately was a tall order.

Bond did his best. As succinctly as he could he told the story of Sum Taeyoung, a South Korean with US and UK university education whose main ambition now was to create as much global chaos as he could to the benefit of his illegal dealings in drugs and armaments. He told the Governor about the chess game, about the deceit as they understood it to be behind the Chinese oil deal to California. He said that security agencies were involved in trying to prevent Taeyoung achieving his plans but he did not name Georgi or the European agency that officially did not exist. It was just too difficult to explain in the short time he had. And he described that, as far as everyone could ascertain, the political terrorist Sum Taeyoung was planning some sort of action specifically against the Governor. As far as they could determine, that was going to be tomorrow, Saturday, but there was some expectation that it could happen at the UN conference today. Nobody could be sure.

Al Williams listened intently and let Bond speak without interruption. Even as he heard himself speaking the words, Bond became more and more disillusioned by what he was saying. How could he expect the Governor to take this seriously when he himself thought what he was saying sounded preposterous and incredulous. But he battled on to the end.

When he was finished, Governor Williams stood and walked around a little as he contemplated what he had been told. Bond waited with growing concern as to how he was going to respond. At last Al Williams walked towards him and said, "Gene. Gene. That's some hell of a story. I don't like saying this but I have to - it sounded like something more from a James Bond spy book rather than from Gene Bond - a trusted environmentalist and friend. It's all a bit hard to take on board - and you haven't offered any substantive evidence."

"The assertion that the oil deal is a falsehood is obviously based on poor information and clearly you don't know the full story. But then, why should you? I'm sorry to be negative - and you're obviously very anxious about this matter. And I certainly don't want to appear rude or unappreciative. But there are so many anomalies in your story and such lack of substantive evidence. But - because it's you - I will report what you have told me to my security people. As you may have noted, there's one hell of a lot of them about here at the moment."

He said the last words with a little laughter in his voice, in marked contrast to his stern stance that had gone before. "All these people - they're keen to see no harm comes to me, Gene. And, you know, they're pretty good at what they do. I trust them - and, after all, it's me that's the target. So if I feel safe it's because of them. But I will report what you have told me. I'm sure they will be more vigilant than ever. It would be helpful if you could let me have this in writing, with any evidence you can provide."

He extended his hand towards Bond. This was clearly a final handshake to denote the end of their meeting.

"It's been good to see you Gene. I'm not sure this time what your message is all about but it's always good to see you."

And with that he escorted Bond back into the room where his team was assembled.

"Of course," he continued "I've got a lot on my mind this morning. An historic day Gene - and all that. Will you be at the conference?"

"Sadly I haven't a ticket sir," Bond responded.

"What about the Party on the Lake?"

"I don't know about that sir," replied Bond.

"Apparently there's a celebration party on the Lake tomorrow morning," Williams told him. "I don't know much about it either. I haven't had my official invitation yet. We've only recently been told about it. But I can get you a ticket for that if you like, and for the conference this afternoon. You should be there. You can be part of my team. It would be appalling if you were to come all the way here and then not attend what we think is such an historic moment. Celia will sort the paperwork and the passes."

"That's fantastic and very generous." responded Bond. And with that, he was led out of the room. He headed back to his own hotel thinking he had done his best but it had not been good enough by a long way. It had been a pretty futile effort. Al Williams had been polite and considerate, but clearly thought the warning unnecessary. Understandably his mind was utterly preoccupied by the speech he was soon to make. For him to take seriously this cock and bull story from an Englishman he had met once was too much to have hoped for. Bond felt annoyed and frustrated. He had let himself and the team down but, more importantly, he had let Governor Al Williams down too. But there was a major element of compensation - access to the conference this afternoon.

With a growing sense of despondency, anxiety and foreboding, Bond checked his watch. There were now only around 24 hours to midday Saturday.

Chapter 25

After leaving the Governor, Bond phoned Georgi to tell him the news about getting the passes. But his calls were unanswered. They did not even go to voice mail. After a few failed attempts, Bond decided if he was to join the UN delegates for lunch it would be too much of a rush to go back to his hotel and then return to the lakeside and the Convention Centre. So he strolled somewhat aimlessly around the small mountainside town of Montreux. He had a couple of hours before the afternoon session at the UN event and it was a chance to see the picturesque town that he had not been to before. But his mind was not on behaving like a tourist and he found himself being pulled as if by a magnet back towards the Convention Centre. By now it had attracted an enormous media frenzy as journalists from all over the world tried to capture the moment Governor Al Williams took the State of California out of the Union. He was pleased he had decided not want to enter the building until closer to the time Al Williams was to speak so he wandered along the lakeside path to where he eventually found an empty bench to sit on.

There he contemplated his meeting with Al Williams and time and time again ran it through his mind. Could he have done anything differently, anything better? He remonstrated with himself at the lack of real success but ultimately concluded it was probably an impossible mission from the outset. At least he could now be in the UN event and see if anything happened there.

His contemplation was interrupted by a call to his mobile phone. It was Jane in Wapping.

"Gene, we have a major problem. Georgi is in the hands of the Americans."

"Jesus!" exclaimed Bond.

"He's under military arrest. It's only just happened and we don't know the detail yet. We know his arrest will come to nothing in the long term but in the meantime he's out of the game."

"Bloody hell!" Bond responded. A mixture of dismay and anger grew in him. He had thought Georgi was being irresponsible in doing what he set out to do. But as the amateur in the team, Bond had no means of stopping him. Now they were in deep trouble.

"We know he's being escorted to Geneva Airport sometime later today and will be accompanied back to the UK. There'll be some questioning but we'll eventually get him out of it."

"Jesus!" repeated Bond.

"It means you're on your own," Jane told him, pointing out the obvious which had already become so nerve shatteringly apparent to Bond. "It's too late to get any help out to you."

There was a silence between them.

"We're still focusing on the chess game here," Jane eventually continued. "And we've also had a report from Williams' team in Geneva that the Governor has been invited to an event on the lake tomorrow."

"I know," Bond told her. "It's the Party on the Lake."

"How do you know about that?" she asked and Bond told her about his meeting with Al Williams, an event which he summarised as probably being just short of a waste of time except for the passes to the UN afternoon session and to the celebration on the lake tomorrow. He did not know what he expected Williams to do, having heard what he had to tell him, but the Governor was obviously very preoccupied by demands to deliver his historic speech. Bond looked at his watch.

"I still think Sum Taeyoung might try something there - in the conference room," Jane told him. "That's despite us thinking the checkmate moment he's planned is tomorrow, at 1200. But I wouldn't be surprised if Sum doesn't pull some stunt during the speech. It's too good a high profile event to miss."

Again there was a pause between them.

"You will have to be our eyes Gene" she said. "And if you go to Georgi's room, unless that's been raided by now, there's some kit there that should be useful. Hopefully he hasn't said anything to anyone so maybe his room will still be intact. Mind you, you've probably been spotted around town with Georgi. That makes an interesting question. How come, people might ask, someone who they now have under military arrest is the chum of someone who is a buddy of the Governor? Unravel that one!"

And she went on to tell Bond what kit there might be in Georgi's room and how to use it. Between them they devised some sort of a plan for the afternoon and the following day, though it could hardly be called a plan, so little did they know about Sum Taeyoung's intentions.

"It seems to me," said Bond as they came towards the end of their deliberations, "that 1200 tomorrow is the key moment according to the chess game. But we might be wrong so it's prudent for me to go to see Al speak this afternoon though God knows what I could do if he's attacked there. Sometime before then I'm told an invitation to the party will be delivered to me. That might show some sort of programme for what's going to happen on the lake. Maybe we'll learn something from that."

And on that hardly positive or decisive note, they concluded the call.

Checking his watch again, Bond decided he just about had enough time to go to Georgi's room now to see if he could find what Jane had told him should be there. It was best to do that while attention gathered on the Convention Centre. He eventually arrived at Georgi's hotel room without encountering anyone and entered with some degree of trepidation. Fortunately he had already got a key to the room as Georgi had thought it prudent they should each have a copy of the other's room key.

As far as Bond could tell, Georgi's room had not come under any sort of search though Georgi was hardly a tidy domestic person. It was difficult to see if the room had been turned over by anyone or if this was Georgi's normal domestic chaos. On a mainly gut feel, Bond felt the room had not been disturbed by outsiders. That was endorsed when Bond found the equipment Jane had talked about. He spent some time getting accustomed to it and tested it, making contact again with Jane as he did so.

By the time he got back to his own room an envelope had been slid under the door. He quickly opened it to find an official invitation to The Party on the Lake. There was a timetable of activity. Bond homed in on 1200. Then, according to the schedule, Governor Al Williams would be presented with something to recognise his achievements in taking California into independence. To Bond, it all stacked up. 1200 tomorrow was going to be the crescendo moment. Sum Taeyoung's big play of the cards. But what? That remained the big unanswered question. But he could not be sure. The speech this afternoon was so obviously the highest profile moment. Sum could still strike then.

Chapter 26

Checking into the conference of the United Nations Department of Economic and Social Affairs proved to be easy and quick mainly because anyone who was going to attend was already in the hall. The normal battle between delegates to get registered had long since subsided. The registration desk was manned by a group of uniformed women who may have been rushed earlier in the day but were now looking decidedly redundant with just a few late stragglers like Gene Bond to attend to. The paperwork given to him by Celia proved to be in order and they were exchanged for a delegate's pass which hung from a lanyard.

Access to the conference room itself was challenging not only because the room was in near darkness but because of the sheer number of media present together with their mountains of equipment and cables. Bond could not even hazard a guess as to how many camera lenses pointed towards the distanced stage. It may have been more than 100. A chaos of cameras, cables, and boxes spread across an area just inside the entrance to the conference hall and had to be navigated in the near darkness to get to the few seats that remained empty for delegates.

An enormous stage with a giant screen behind it extended from one side wall to another. On the left of the stage was a lectern with an illuminated DESA logo on it. To the right sat a line of people, three men, one of whom was Al Williams, and two women. One seat was unoccupied and presumably belonged to the person currently speaking at the lectern. This person could also be seen on the screen, his image being projected onto virtually half of it. Bond guessed the picture of the speaker was some six metres square. It was huge but then so was the audience which numbered more than 400. The other half of the screen was occupied by text and graphs that were supporting what the speaker was saying. Spotlights illuminated the lectern, the area where Al Williams sat with the other four people, and provided some creative lighting either side of the enormous screen.

After much difficulty in finding a vacant seat, Bond took stock of the occasion. The room was packed. There seemed not to be an inch unoccupied. Gradually, as he became accustomed to the darkness, he could see dim images of people standing either side of the hall at more or less regular intervals. Security, he wondered? It seemed more than likely. If Sum Taeyoung was going to attempt some sort of attack here it was going to be extremely difficult to see him before it happened. But surely, he tried to convince himself, there were enough skilled professionals around the place to stop him doing anything.

The speaker, who Bond gradually realised was DESA's current chairman, was coming to the end of what Bond guessed had been a long speech worthy of introducing one of the most important speeches in the history of DESA. He was now reminding the audience and the world's media how the organisation had a long and successful history of helping countries meet their economic, social and environmental challenges. The values of sustainable development were, he told the audience, a bedrock within DESA as were concerns about equity and equality.

"In countries large and small," he said, "developed and developing, DESA has a track record of helping people take control of their own destiny. But never before has DESA been involved in furthering the cause of democracy in quite the way it is doing today."

And he went on to talk in detail about how the State of California had approached DESA for support for its ambitions to become an independent state. Bond could sense a tension rising in the room but he wondered if that was restricted to himself and his concerns about Taeyoung's plans, or was it being felt by all the other delegates in anticipation of the forthcoming historic speech by Al Williams? If, Bond had already concluded, the South Korean was to undertake some mischief at this event, it was going to be difficult if not impossible for him, Bond, to do anything about it. It was, he convinced himself, a matter for the security people who surrounded the Governor, not him. Despite being seated in such a packed auditorium he felt very alone and frustratingly limited in what he could do. With Georgi no longer involved and with it being impossible to communicate with Jane because of the closeness of people sitting around him, Bond felt pretty helpless. If Taeyoung was to strike now, it would be up to others to deal with him.

At last the Chairman of DESA reached the end of his contribution and welcomed Governor Al Williams to the stage. Delegates rose from their chairs and, as a demonstration of diplomatic courtesy, gave the Californian a standing ovation. The conference room was now full of emotion and the atmosphere was electric. Bond looked around him, not able to see much through the mass of people, but with a growing nervousness now that Al Williams was out at the front of the stage, before the audience, and a clear target.

"I am here representing some 40 million Americans," Al Williams told the audience in Montreux and those watching and listening via television and radio around the world. "Californian Americans", he added.

"And whatever happens here today, and what may happen in the future, nothing can alter the fact that Californians are Americans. Neither can we be accused of being traitors to our forefathers or to those who gave their lives in bloody conflict that ultimately resulted in the formation of the United States. What course we set upon today cannot be identified as anti-American or anti-USA. It is not. This matter is singularly about the practicalities of providing an effective, democratic, accessible and understanding administration that can truly represent and respond to the interests, concerns, needs and wishes of 40 million people."

A pause for effect and, unknown to the audience, for Al Williams to grab control of his nerves which had been at breaking point. Now they were coming more under his control. In contrast, Bond was deeply impressed. The speech was being delivered in a strong and measured tone and was, he felt, very statesmanlike.

"Inherent within this is our belief that many democratic administrations are no longer fit for purpose. Providing an effective and dynamic mechanism for the

320 million or more citizens of the United States of America creates stresses and strains that inhibit the process to such a degree it ultimately becomes ineffective. It can also become dangerously distanced from the very people it was designed to serve."

"That is what we believe has happened in America. Our people in California feel distanced and disconnected from the administration that manages us. That has impacted on those who participate in the democratic process. Their numbers have dwindled. Disillusionment has led to apathy and even hostile antagonism. We are in danger of opening the door and giving an open invitation to extreme minority groups. That potentially leads the democratic process into very perilous territory."

He paused to let his message sink in.

"I stand before you representing 40 million citizens. That is a number almost four times the size of the population of Belgium. It is nearly twice the size of the population of Australia. It is bigger than Canada. We have an economy which, according to some league tables, is the eighth largest in the world, just behind Brazil, Russia and Italy and bigger than India, Canada, Australia, Spain and Mexico. We are of a size to be a truly viable and secure entity that can make a proper contribution to the family of nations that is the UN. But we also believe it essential we are administrated by a management that properly connects to us, understands us and is accessible. That is why the people of California have, through a proper democratic process, voted to become masters of their own destiny."

Applause rippled through the audience. Al Williams paused, looked into the blackness caused by the spotlights shining straight at him, and tried to ensure his audience felt he was speaking to them on an individual basis, even if he could not see any one of them.

He continued. "The people of California have spoken. In an honest, legal and binding referendum they have declared their desire to manage their own affairs."

And he told his audience how this would happen, the practical steps that had already been taken and the role of DESA in the process to date. His speech was forceful but spoken by a man who had total belief in the message he was delivering. Bond thought it was inspiring though while Williams was on the stage his mind was as much concerned for the man's safety as it was on what he was saying.

It was a faultless performance. At the end, the audience rose and applauded at length and with genuine enthusiasm. Governor Williams joined the Chairman of DESA at a desk that had been brought onto the stage and the two men signed official documents that recorded the proceedings of the day.

The whole session lasted nearly two hours. Bond was relieved when it was all over and Al Williams had been safely escorted away from the conference room. Bond was unable to see him leave the Convention Centre but with no dramas unfolding he, as last, was able to link up with Jane.

"Some speech," she said.

"Yes," agreed Bond. "And safely delivered."

"So it leaves us with Taeyoung's checkmate move at tomorrow's party."

"Looks that way," agreed Bond. And they agreed to link up again early the following morning.

Chapter 27

His watch showed it was 0803. He was acutely aware that less than four hours remained until the anticipated Taeyoung showdown yet they still did not know what it was or how it would happen.

This was much in Bond's mind as he sat on a bench on the pathway alongside Lake Geneva. It was a bright morning, very still. The Lake looked like a mirror. The mountain massifs on the opposite side of the Lake were reflected upside down so clearly in the lake it was hard to tell where reflection met reality.

To his left, a few hundred metres away, one of the 16 Belle Epoque paddle steamers that sail the lakes of Switzerland was roped to the jetty ready to receive passengers for the Party on the Lake. Nearly 80 metres long, steel plated and with the capacity to take well over 1,000 passengers, today's pride of Switzerland would accommodate less than 300 visitors but also its crew, a large catering contingent, a military band and countless security people.

Bond had been here from just before seven o'clock, as well prepared after a sleepless night for the day ahead as he felt he could be, but full of doubts, worries and concerns that, somehow, the responsibility for the events to follow now fell to him, virtually on his own. He had reflected time and time again on how this had come about, and the more he thought about it the more he got angry with Georgi's reckless irresponsibility.

He had determined to be early to see the boat arrive. He wanted to know as much as he could about everything before the clock neared 1200. There was no paddle steamer at the jetty when he sat down on the bench but there was a general buzz of activity on the nearby water as countless small boats scurried around. Bond had not bothered to count them but there was a good many, a mix of rigid inflatables and high speed cabin cruisers. Some were clearly from the Swiss police, some from the Swiss army. Bond could see one carried the insignia of the

Royal Navy and the others, which he could not identify, were mostly the rigids. He assumed one way or another they were American. It was quite a flotilla.

He had seen the elaborate security precautions that had been evident from the start. Even before the paddle steamer was in sight, a large group of military people had undertaken a meticulous security sweep of the area around the jetty which was now cordoned off with a high portable metal fence but with a small gap through which visitors would pass but only after their credentials had been carefully scrutinised and a quick body scan undertaken with a hand held scanner. Everything being carried aboard was meticulously inspected. The paddle steamer arrived trailing black smoke from its funnel as it edged towards the jetty. Once it had been roped fore and aft, a security team including three sniffer dogs set about searching the vessel from top to bottom.

Bond had watched it all with a growing sense of excitement and tension. He was still feeling uncomfortable with the translucent earpiece in his left ear. Through it he hoped to hear the voice of Jane back in Wapping. And from the high powered but tiny button microphone on his lapel, he also hoped to speak to her. In fact, they had already tested the kit several times. It had worked. And it had not only provided a bit of reassurance to Bond but also the joyous news from Jane with which to start this testing day. Nagriza was making improvement at the Birmingham hospital. It raised his spirits though the good news had the caveat that she remained very poorly. She was conscious and was taking food and drink but remained in the intensive care unit. But these were now hopeful signs at least.

For the umpteenth time Bond looked at his invitation. It was from Asian Pacific Trading Inc and personally signed by Jake Bloomer. It showed the boarding time to be from 0930 through to no later than 1015, a sailing time of 1030, a drinks reception, an early buffet lunch commencing at 1130, a presentation to be made to Governor Williams at 1200. The boat would return to the jetty at around 1430.

His watch now showed 0911. Amongst the bustle of activity around the quayside, two tall, dark suited gentlemen arrived by the gap in the security fence. It was clear from the reaction of those around them that they were important and key elements of the day's event and, as one or two very early guests arrived, it also became clear they were the reception committee. Bond called up Jane and described the two.

After a pause, Jane's voice came back loud and clear to his earpiece.

"We're pretty sure one is Jake Bloomer and we think the other is Jo Summers. Both APTI people. Jake is its top man."

At 0930 the band launched into action, playing a repertoire of light music.

Bond decided to go aboard. This was a worry and a panic for him because he thought the security check might find his radio link to Jane. She said she thought that was unlikely. Georgi's kit was pretty sophisticated and incorporated anti-surveillance elements. That did not stop Bond building up a sweat of worry as he walked as deliberately as he could towards the jetty. He should not have been concerned. He chose his moment to coincide with the arrival of a group of about 15 other visitors so the security check area was quite busy. In the end it was all a bit of an anti-climax and he passed through with no response from the body search, shaking hands with the two APTI men who beamed at him in welcome though obviously had no idea who he was.

The paddle steamer was bigger than Bond had expected and only its upper deck was opened for The Party on the Lake. When Bond got there he saw that a long table had been set up in the middle of the aft deck with a stand radio microphone alongside. To either side other tables stood in wait for the arrival of the buffet. The area was becoming busier all the time as more and more guests assembled on the paddle steamer. Bond wandered over to the side of the ship that was adjacent the jetty and stood watching events. He had not long positioned himself here when he saw a black truck arrive, a highly polished and gleaming example of what would be called a Utility in Australia or Canada. With its grumbling V8 engine just ticking over it progressed cautiously along the pathway to park right next to the gap in the security fence. Two burly men got out of the cabin and retrieved a large box from the back of the truck. It was obviously weighty as they struggled to carry it towards the boat. They walked towards the gap for visitors and Jake Bloomer stepped forward to greet them. He patted the first man on the shoulder in welcome and, from his various gesticulations, instructed him where to take the box. The two men proceeded onto the boat and in a short time came into view on the stern deck. They placed the box by the side of the stand microphone, unclipped its lid, and departed.

It was not long after that the band suddenly stopped playing mid tune. Bond looked towards the arrival point just in time to see Al Williams approaching the boat with an escort of about 20 people. There was much handshaking and laughter as the group moved through the security check and on board. As they did so, the military band burst into life playing 'I Love You California' which Bond later found to be the State's – the new independent nation's - official song. Maybe, he thought, it was now the National Anthem.

Bond checked his watch again and saw it was 1020. As he did so, a rumble of noise and trembling down the length of the boat heralded the start of the paddles and, spot on time at 1030, the steamer left the jetty with a whoop from its funnel that echoed round the lakeside part of Montreux.

"Tell me what you see," Jane called to Bond. "Be our eyes."

Bond did his best. It was not easy. The area was quite busy now. The boat was curving a route out into the lake, its flotilla of accompanying craft bustling around in seemingly complete disorder. The blue stillness of the lake was churned into a spray of flying silver water. Bond made the comment to Jane that it looked more like 'uncoordinated chaos' than an organised military flotilla and assumed that was because of the numbers of different agencies involved. It all looked a bit confused to Bond but he felt sure the professionals had everything well in hand.

He recalled the confidence with which Al Williams had talked about the security around him.

By 1100 white attired staff started to assemble the buffet. It was clear that the plan was for the eating and drinking to continue right through to 1430 when the boat got back to Montreux with only the formalities at 1200 interrupting The Party on the Lake.

Bond wandered around, nodding to people but trying to avoid being dragged into any meaningless pleasantries. He had too much on his mind, too much to be alert for, too much to report back to Jane as often as he could.

"Can you see anything out of the ordinary?" Jane pestered him. Bond told her he wasn't that accustomed to receptions on paddle steamers so wasn't sure what could be termed "out of the ordinary."

"It's all out of the bloody ordinary as far as I'm concerned," he told her.

By 1130, Al Williams, Celia, others he recognised from having seen them in Al Williams' hotel room, and the two APTI men, assembled themselves in little groups not far from the table and the stand microphone, ready for the coming formalities and the presentation to the Governor.

Bond sensed a growing feeling of excitement. It was obviously not something others were conscious of but he knew it was now only 30 minutes to Sum Taeyoung's threatened moment. His checkmate. Bond's sense of frustration and anxiety was reaching screaming point when, at just before 1145, Jane's voice crackled into his ear.

"Bond. Bond. Stand by." He had never heard her voice sound so urgent. "We've a message coming in from the US Embassy in Bern. It's - it's - you must be fucking joking" - she was now clearly talking to someone in Wapping. "Bond!" she called again. "Bond. Listen carefully. The UK Embassy in Bern has just received a hand written note from Governor Al Williams. It's a suicide note! Do you hear me? A suicide note from Al Williams! We are assessing it now. Assessing implications for you out there."

The line went silent. Bond was having difficulty comprehending what she had said.

"Bond. The letter says in the light of his …."

Her voice turned to speak to others in Wapping. Clearly she was dealing with a huge flow of information both coming in to her and going out.

"….it says – "because of my abject failure of the people of California, I have had no alternative but to take the action I have taken …….." Oh shit! Stand by Gene."

The silence was brief.

"Gene. Gene. Our analysts here reckon they're going to blow up your boat - the steamer! Gene. Do you hear? Do you understand? Taeyoung's going to blow up the paddle steamer! Can you see how the hell he might do that?"

As she was speaking, with Bond's watch now at 1149, he saw Jake Bloomer take an envelope from his pocket and hand it to Al Williams. At the same time, Jo Summers was undoing the box that had earlier been carried aboard. As he watched, Bond saw him take the lid off then, with the help of another man, lift an object from the box. It was large, probably a metre and a half tall, stark black and standing on a plinth. It was a chess piece. It was a Black Queen!

Bond looked back at Al Williams who had extracted a letter from the envelope he had been given by Jake Bloomer. Standing as he was some 10 paces away from the Governor, Bond saw that he had gone white. The blood had drained from his face.

As Bond watched, horrified and mesmerised by what he was seeing, Al Williams' legs gave out on him and he grabbed at Jake Bloomer, the nearest person to him, for support. Bond's earpiece exploded into life again.

"Gene - how many inflatables are there on the lake?" It was Jane again, shouting down the line.

"What?" Bond said without thinking about what she was saying. His mind was racing and was elsewhere than logged into Jane. He hadn't even answered her last question yet. And he had not told her what he had seen. He had not told Wapping about the Black Queen. His watch now showed 1155. There was a new and nagging thought in his mind and he could not quite catch it.

"Bond. Bond. Count the inflatables."

"What?" he responded again. But his mind was not on what she was saying. There was something in his memory that he couldn't quite grasp but he knew it was important.

"Count the fucking inflatables!" Jane's voice rasped at him.

But he was desperately trying to hang on to the thread of a thought that was developing. He had sat on the bench and watched before the boat had arrived, whilst it was loaded, then as people boarded. Everything and everyone had been checked, searched and body searched. Everything - apart from one item!

With Jane's voice still bellowing in his ear, Bond looked at the Black Queen. It was a big item in itself - and there was the plinth too. Bond convinced himself. It was the only thing on board that had not been security checked. The revelation in his mind translated into instinctive action. He dived for the chess piece, surprising everyone by his move but ahead of anyone being able to stop him. This was no carefully planned move by Bond. It was pure reaction fuelled by adrenalin. And he had virtually completed the action before anyone tried to restrain him.

Thinking back afterwards, it was one of those moments so packed with action it was as if time slowed. He remembered grabbing the Black Queen from the table, was instantly horrified by its weight. Under normal circumstances he would never have been able to lift it very high by himself. But the adrenalin was pumping through his veins at high pressure giving him extra strength. As officials, guests, security people and others looked on in sheer disbelief, Bond lifted the Black Queen high enough to tip her over the nearby railing and overboard. A few people who had been standing near the Black Queen tried to stop Bond as soon as he swung into action but Bond was ahead of them all. Now, as the chess piece disappeared over the side and headed towards the water, they turned their attention to securing the perpetrator of the deed. Even as they did so, with Jane's voice now screaming in his earpiece, Bond heard a new sound enter his world. From close by, on the lake side of the paddle steamer, the sound of a high powered marine engine roaring into full throttle was getting closer.

Pulled down by the hands that had grabbed him, he had just hit the highly polished wooden afterdeck when there was a mighty explosion. Onlookers afterwards said it was as if a depth charge had gone off. The Black Queen had only just hit the lake when it exploded in a massive eruption that sent a column of water high into the air. The stern of the sizeable paddle steamer thrust upwards, momentarily hanging some 10 metres out of the water, then crashing down with a huge thwack into Lake Geneva, sending an enormous fountain of water and crash wave out from the scene. Anyone standing on board at the moment of the explosion and sudden thrust of the boat was thrown from their feet. Almost immediately there was another loud crack, then another, then the "ratatat" of a machine gun being fired.

From where he lay Bond looked around. There were bodies everywhere, mostly still alive and recovering from having been thrown to the deck when the bomb exploded. The gun fire was definitely concentrated on his area of the boat and was creating carnage. Bits of metal, woodwork and even fragments of body parts were flying in all directions. Smoke was starting to drift through the scene and was gathering in thickness. He saw that Al Williams was separated from him by one other person. Ruthlessly he pushed that other person aside and as best he could grabbed the Governor by the arm.

Al Williams looked at him vacantly.

"Sir - we've got to move!" Bond screamed at him but got no response. Deciding there and then that there was no more time for words, he grabbed the Governor and pulled him across the deck. Two of his group tried to intervene but Bond shouted at them "get him inside" and was relieved when they turned from trying to keep him away from Williams to now helping move the stricken politician.

All the time the carnage around them grew worse. Bullets from the machine gun were ripping the aft deck to pieces and it was now littered with bits of timber, brass, and body parts. The acrid black smoke added to the chaos. The sound of gunfire was now accompanied by loud thuds as what Bond took to be grenades landed on the deck. Behind all this, Bond could hear what sounded like a full-scale maritime battle raging on the lake.

The three of them successfully dragged Williams to the staircase and bumped him unceremoniously down the stairs. The deck they were now on was empty and clearly not a target in the way the upper rear deck was. Bond could see that was now partly on fire. A throat catching smell permeated everywhere, stinging his eyes, making breathing difficult. A smoke mix of cordite, burning wood and whatever explosives Sum had used in his chess piece bomb drifted across the stricken paddle steamer.

"Bond. Come in Bond! What the bloody hell's happening?" Jane's voice was close to being hysterical.

And, as best he could, he told her what had happened in the last few minutes. It took him seemingly an age to do so.

"Bloody hell!" was the only response he got.

It was some time later that Bond realised that during the course of rescuing Al Williams he had somehow grabbed from him the letter he had been given by Jake Summers. It was now torn and gashed and splattered with blood. It had no heading. It read:

To Governor Al Williams of the Independent Nation of California

We congratulate you on your speech of independence. We hope and anticipate that California's move will encourage other states to leave the unruly, arrogant, imperialistic United States of America. The demise of the mighty Soviet Union was unjustly proclaimed to give freedom to people. Clearly the people of the USA need to be freed from the tyranny of its administration. We anticipate your actions will ultimately lead to the full collapse of the USA.

We make no apology for the illusion that helped trigger this historic course of events. There was - and is - no oil from China for California. It was a charade designed to facilitate what we have achieved. We planned this as a military campaign but based on a game of chess. The Black Queen has dominated the game over the months it has taken to execute this plan. Now the last move has been played.

Governor Al Williams. Shah Mat!

Signed

Sum Taeyoung - for those who seek global chaos

And there were four scribbled and not very legible signatures with the words underneath –

For those we remember in the name of Vladimir Lenin, Felix Dzerzhinsky and the Cheka movement.

Chapter 27

The rosehips bloomed either side of the pathway that led to the tea room and the copper samovar from which they would take tea on Tatyshev Island on the Yenisei River near Krasnoyarsk in Eastern Siberia. Viktor Blucher was on his way to meet his three surviving Cheka comrades who were breaking the longstanding rule and adding another meeting to their normal once a year arrangement. He had spoken to all three since they had arrived in the city yesterday, one via the Trans-Siberian Railway into Krasnoyarsk central station, and the other two into the local Emelyanovo airport.

It was a big effort for these four veterans to travel and to meet but this day they had special reason to do so. They had also invited their sponsoring Oligarch to be with them, but he had declined. He too was pleased with the outcome, but too busy to celebrate. They were pleased he had declined.

And this was indeed a celebration for the four old, creaking Chekists. With tea being the only substance they consumed nowadays, they raised their cups in triumph. The break up of the Soviet Union had been avenged. California had left the United States of America. Now they hoped, as had been the domino effect with the Soviet Union, other states would do likewise. They had monitored all the news outputs they could. Levels of discontent across the USA were now at heights never seen before. Two camps of opinion had developed, one supportive of the Californian move and advocating others did the same, and the other diametrically opposed and fighting to maintain the Union. Though no tangible domino effect had yet happened, there was enough noise, especially in the Southern States, to convince the band of four that the rot had well and truly set in. The seeds had been sewn. It was cause for celebration.

In the Insadong district of Seoul, a now not so large, less overweight, smartly suited, clean shaven man with his hair cropped almost to his head, climbed his way quite briskly to the top of the stairs of the Flying Bird Tea Room. He still puffed from the ordeal but far less so than he had done in the recent past. Once seated, he ordered his usual double harmony tea. He was acutely aware that his routine use of the tea shop was a potential breach of his own code of security but he also knew he had created chaos for his enemies through his electronic counter-surveillance measures and his change of physical appearance. Being in the chaos business, these thoughts pleased him sufficiently for him to continue to enjoy the double harmony tea, even if it did offer some risk of his location being exposed. He sat on his own to contemplate recent events, to take stock of what had happened - to make a self-analytical appraisal of his own performance - and to rate the result.

In many regards this project had been a success. Its prime objective had been served. He had caused global chaos and his clients were satisfied. California had left the United States of America and relationships between China and the USA had taken a serious turn for the worse. Across the USA, voices were raised loudly in support of what California had done. In Texas, an already active campaign had gained a new momentum. A new rift was developing between the North and South of America the likes of which had not been seen for around 150 years. To Sum it was most satisfactory.

On the deficit side, Al Williams lived on. In many regards that did not matter but Sum Taeyoung was annoyed with himself that he had put his name to the letter that had been handed to Williams. The element of the plan in which the paddle steamer would sink, taking Governor Williams and the evidence with it, had failed. That niggled at Sum Taeyoung big time. It festered within him like a cancer. He did not like failure, in any degree. Now he would have to make a balanced judgement as to whether to write that episode off as one of ill fortune or bad execution by his troops, or seek revenge from those who had thwarted his plan. The name 'Bond' hung heavily on his mind as a major element of the plan that had gone wrong in its execution.

As he supped his tea, at this particular moment he remained undecided as to whether to close this project or to treat it as unfinished business. Bond, perhaps, was still classified as work in hand.

In California all hell broke loose once it was realised that Al Williams had been duped by a scam. There was no Chinese oil and never had been. Efforts to track down APTI came to a dead end, literally because its main human components were dead, having been cut down by machine gun fire in what one Californian paper called the Great Lake Geneva Gun Boat Battle.

Al Williams had, of course, immediately resigned and did his best to escape media attention. Stressed to the point of near breakdown, he went into a medical institute for a while to receive counselling. His political career was smashed and he was never again seen in public life.

Perhaps to the surprise of many, the Referendum decision, having already been declared, and with California constitutionally removed from the United States, was maintained. Across the USA the debate raged, with anti Washington fever gaining particular strength across the Southern States. President Jack Thompson became the focus of a bloody political battle with many of his own party accusing him of failure in stopping the California events happening. Now a great divide, entrenched in historic differences that many had thought to be dead, buried and long forgotten, resurfaced with new interpretations of issues that had split the population in historic events of the past. The gap between those who have and those who have not reinvigorated the work of ngo organisations and activists. The taboo of white versus black began to be openly debated again. As had happened in the past the North and the South were again at loggerheads. This widening divide with its echoes into American history were greeted with great satisfaction in Krasnoyarsk and Seoul.

In Wapping, Georgi Patarava had recently returned from Brussels where he had had to face up to a severe reprimand from the masters of the European spy operation that does not officially exist. As a key element of it he had his knuckles rapped for a major breach of professionalism. He had allowed - at a crucial moment in a project - a non-professional combatant to become their first line operator in the field. It was unheard of. It was a huge breach of discipline.

Now, gathered in the basement in Wapping were Georgi, Bond, Jane, Jamie, Alan and, fresh out of hospital but still looking very groggy, Nagriza. Nearly a month had passed since the battle on Lake Geneva. Bond, identified by many as the hero of the hour for throwing what was now known to be a substantial bomb off the paddle steamer and thereby saving significant numbers of lives, was also an enigma that the authorities did not know how to handle. Bond had been retained for a while in Montreux police station where it was made clear to him he was not being 'held' as such and was 'free to go whenever he liked.' Not knowing where quite to go to, he had stayed where he was until he was eventually whisked away by staff from the British Consulate General in Geneva. Whilst treating him with high respect for being the saviour of the day, they immediately served him with a Writ, actionable should he break any element of the Officials Secrets Act.

"I haven't a clue what this means," Bond told the very young, very well spoken lady who had served it upon him.

"I haven't a bloody clue either," she admitted. "Basically I think it means your Queen and your country expect you to keep your mouth zipped." She advised him to do the same to the hoard of media and officials from a wide variety of government agencies that were trying to get at him.

"If anyone gets upperty about that, you tell me," she added.

"I won't hesitate," Bond promised.

The media attention over the next few days was intense. Rumours started to fly that a British spy, unbelievably called Bond, was the hero of the Great Lake Geneva Gun Boat Battle. He had saved many, many lives including that of Al Williams, by throwing a bomb off the paddle steamer. The press went apoplectic that they were not getting access to the English hero, a genuine Bond. It was the sort of event that makes huge columns of press coverage and that is what it did, though much, apart from what had physically been witnessed at Montreux, was speculation.

What was known was that someone - thought to be an Englishman named Bond - had lobbed a bomb off the paddle steamer an instant before it had exploded. At the same time, a high powered rigid inflatable boat, marked with US Navy Seal colours, had opened fire on the paddle steamer with a fixed, high velocity machine gun. Two others guns on board were targeted at other security boats and had created bedlam.

"Fourteen people on board the paddle steamer were killed and 22 injured," reported Georgi. "Jake Bloomer and Jo Summers were amongst the dead. They had clearly been specific targets. Amongst the security boats on the lake, four people were killed including the three terrorists in the inflatable. Eight others were injured."

"Sum Taeyoung's plot was to dislodge California from the United States. To do that, he set up a company called APTI which, through some clever disguising and quite a lot of palming of the hands of corrupt Chinese officials, had all the appearances of being a Chinese procurement agency. In fact, amazingly, it did start to trade in oil, but only enough so that if California tested the situation they would be able to respond."

"Sum's plan was timed to the minute. Sadly for him, luckily for us, a few things went a bit astray. What was supposed to happen was that Jake Summers was to hand Williams a letter just before the bomb in the Black Queen was triggered. The letter told Williams he had been caught in a massive, sophisticated, scam. The letter was signed by Sum Taeyoung and four Russians."

"Who on earth were the Russians?" asked Jamie.

"We've traced them to what we think to be a group of retired Russian military. Or, to be more precise, former senior secret service officers of the Soviet Union. They seem to be some sort of revenge group."

"Revenging what?" queried Jane.

"The demise of the Soviet Union," Georgi told her. "There's an old school of military people right across the former Soviet empire that thinks it shouldn't have been disbanded. There's not much they can do about that - except perhaps scowl and sulk. But this group seems to have somehow got active - and to have found money by which to fund Taeyoung's scheme."

"At around the same time as the Black Queen was due to be exploded, a letter was supposed to be delivered to the US Embassy in Switzerland. We think that happened a bit earlier than was planned by Taeyoung. It should have been exactly at the same time as the bomb went off but it was a bit early, which is why you were able to relay it on to Gene before the Black Queen exploded. It was supposed to be a letter from Al Williams saying he had killed himself in shame."

"How did Sum know Williams was going to commit suicide?" asked Bond.

"He didn't - and, as far as we know, Williams wasn't going to anyway," Georgi told him. "But Sum expected Williams to die when the ship blew up. So the issue of suicide would have become irrelevant. Williams should have died anyway. But the letter, a forgery allegedly from Williams, said he was going to. It was another way by which Taeyoung could publicly shame Al Williams and cause further chaos."

Georgi paused for a drink.

"Sum had a belt and braces action plan. He expected Williams and his APTI colleagues to go down with the paddle steamer. While it was important Williams died, it was critical to Taeyoung that his APTI people also died so he could close down that route to him. It was vital to him that he couldn't be traced. And he couldn't just hope that they would go down with the boat, even if it was highly likely. So he bought in a killer squad that disguised itself as a US Navy Seal team. As you noticed Gene, there were lots of boats on the lake that day and we don't think anyone had a clear idea of what was going on, what agencies were there, or who was in command. It was a military mess."

"It certainly seemed that way to me," Bond agreed.

"Anyway," continued Georgi "It was Sum's boat crew who were supposed to ensure Summers and Bloomer died. And they did. Where he made a mistake - and we're all liable to make them now and then as I know to my current pain - was to sign the letter to Al Williams. Of course, he expected it would go down with the boat, together with the mystery as to whether or not Al Williams had, or would have, committed suicide."

"So, did Sum Taeyoung win?" asked Nagriza.

"Yes, mostly he did. His plot to dislodge California from the USA succeeded. His crescendo moment - his checkmate moment on Lake Geneva - missed the mark. So, maybe I give Sum 8 out of 10. Not bad."

"What about us?" queried Jamie.

"Not too good really. We didn't stop Sum's main plot. We got that wrong. We stopped the checkmate finale, but mainly through Gene here. And your boss is in the shit with his bosses. So, maybe 5 out of 10. Not so good."

"I assume Sum Taeyoung is as good as being a dead man?" Bond asked of Georgi.

"He should be," responded Georgi but from his tone of voice something was obviously wrong.

"You got a problem?" asked Bond.

Georgi rubbed his chin in a sign of exasperation. "He should be as good as a dead man - but right now I don't know where he is," he replied. He was obviously highly embarrassed having to make this confession.

Bond was puzzled. "But here - with all the technology you showed off - you said could find him anywhere. Whenever you wanted to. You said you could now find the needle in the haystack."

"I did," agreed Georgi, in some discomfort and embarrassment.

"So what's happened?"

"He's disappeared," confessed Georgi. "Somehow he's shaken off our electronic surveillance. He's not been back to his office in Seoul - as far as we know. Somehow he's changed his profile. We've done everything we can to find him. So, I have to confess to you, we've failed. Somehow, maybe just for the moment, Sum Taeyoung has vanished!"

A silence fell on the group. Bond could feel their gloom. It had not been a good operation. Eventually it was Nagriza who broke it with something she asked of Bond.

"And what about you Gene? You're the only one to come out of this well. So, what happens to you now?"

It was a question Bond had been dreading. He had had difficulty in answering the question for himself let alone from anyone else, especially Nagriza. He was so relieved to see her out of hospital. Clearly she was far from being one hundred per cent recovered. She could hardly walk and was breathless most of the time. She should have stayed in hospital longer but had signed herself out. As soon as he had seen her the emotional stirrings had started again. Bond had never encountered a woman like this before and the memories of her - especially in his bed in Birmingham - remained fresh in his mind. His answer had not been pre-planned. He was so drawn to her, yet she came with so much baggage.

"I have been pulled into something over the last few months that I didn't plan, didn't want, and at no time felt comfortable with. You say I have come out of this

OK while you lot consider you have failed. In my analysis, my life has changed completely and not for the better. It will never be the same again. It will take a long time before the media interest dies away - maybe never. I hugely resent that. But I will have to learn to live with it."

"As a group of people I hold you in high regard and my friendship with you, Georgi, remains as strong as ever though I will never forgive you for your crazy act in Switzerland."

He turned to Nagriza. There was a great deal of emotion in his voice and he struggled to get the words out without choking.

"I think you are a stunning lady, Nagriza, and an exceptional person. I have loved being with you. You know that."

"But, the world you have dragged me into, which is going to be difficult to escape from, which has a media pack chasing me everywhere - it's not my world. It's a world that belongs in fiction. It's a shame it can't stay in fiction because a lot of people have been very hurt in recent weeks. I have lived a horror story in recent months. I want to get back to my normality - to do my work which I think is important. It's certainly important to me. So, knowing that I have all sorts of secrecy documents to sign and that, no doubt, I will be under some sort of surveillance from now on, I think it's time to go my own way. To have a beer with you now and then, Georgi. To see you sometime Nagriza."

He stood up from the glass table around which they had been talking and went and shook their hands one by one. It became the inevitable bear hug with Georgi and a long, lingering kiss with Nagriza. Then Bond left, leaving one mad world behind him and returning to another, equally mad.

Some points of reference for the factual elements of the book

- Professor Tony Marmont (Brian Kemp in the book) see:

http://www.independent.co.uk/life-style/profiletony-marmontenergy-secrets-of-a-highflyer-1570297.html
http://www.airfuelsynthesis.com/about-us/tony-marmont/tonys-blog/viewtag/16.html

- PURE Project on Isle of Unst

http://pureenergycentre.com/

- World Business Council for Sustainable Development (video of its President, Peter Bakker, speaking to HRH Prince Charles and an audience of financial directors in St James's Palace).

http://www.wbcsd.org/Pages/EDocument/EDocumentDetails.aspx?ID=15305&NoSearchContextKey=true

- The Global Warming Policy Foundation

www.thegwpf.org/

The Stockholm Resilience Centre
http://www.stockholmresilience.org/

- WWF One Planet Living

http://wwf.panda.org/what_we_do/how_we_work/conservation/one_planet_living/

Printed in Great Britain
by Amazon.co.uk, Ltd.,
Marston Gate.